What p
DEATH OF THE YELLOW SWAN:

I'm openly, unabashedly a fan of Steven Roth. I read everything he writes, usually start to finish in one sitting so that I can immerse myself completely in whatever scenario he presents. This is a particularly interesting series. I'm a huge fan of Art Deco, Film Noir, and historical accuracy. ALL of these are present in this book, with the noir setting of the entire novel taking me somewhere I want to go. I decided to try reading this in pieces, which resulted in my missing my subway stop on several days. So, I have to just suck it up, and slurp the book down, and admit I have a problem. I'm already looking forward to whatever Mr. Roth has in store for us for the next book. Read and enjoy. On a side note, I'm dumbfounded that his books are not being made into movies. The plots warrant it.....all of them.

—PP

What people are saying about
DEATH IN THE FLOWERY KINGDOM:

I am a dyed-in-the-wool aficionado of author Steven M. Roth and his brilliant detective novels. This time, Steve Roth turned the tables on me by taking his readers to Shanghai, China, year 1935, via **DEATH IN THE FLOWERY KINGDOM**. We are introduced to a fascinating old school, Chinese Inspector Detective Sun-Jin. The reader is immersed in several clashing Chinese cultures.

I am impressed with author Steven Roth's meticulous

research and well-crafted descriptions. I could place myself on the streets of Shanghai as the author forms engrossing word pictures in his description of Shanghai in the 1930s. Mr. Roth's clear writing style helps the reader negotiate the twists and turns of the compelling plots and sub-plots of every one of his brilliant detective novels.

—WJC

What people are saying about
NO PLACE TO HIDE:

NO PLACE TO HIDE is a tense, beautifully sculpted novel that blends international politics, the military, and of course crime. . . .When an author is able to strike a chord of fear with the opening lines, the reader can be assured the designated genre of 'suspense novel' is correct. Steve does this with direct ease. . . . . And [after this opening], we're off and running and that [fast, tense] pace is sustained throughout this fine book. . . .Reading this second installment of the Trace Austin series develops a need to read the entire series — and that is a solid sign that Steven M. Roth is a novelist of significance.

—Grady Harp, AMAZON HALL OF
FAME TOP 50 REVIEWER

What people are saying about
NO SAFE PLACE:

Steven Roth has written a terrifyingly real bioweapon suspense novel. He has the chops to keep a reader turning pages and anxious about what comes next. *No Safe Place* alerts us to what the government has done and may still be doing to an unsuspecting and unconcerned public. Highly recommended.

—Charlie Stella
Author of *TOMMY RED* and eight other crime novels

What people are saying about
MANDARIN YELLOW

A splendidly told and sophisticated tale by a first-time novelist. The multi-layered murder mystery not only remains engaging throughout, but also offers the reader a superb primer on Chinese culture and history, particularly post-World War II history.

If you're a mystery fan, you shouldn't miss this novel that features a Parker Duofold (the eponymous Mandarin Yellow). This is prime mystery: well plotted and compellingly written. Roth weaves a taut storyline, paces it perfectly, and wraps it in twists and turns that make no sense until you get to the end (when everything clicks perfectly into place). Along the way, he slips in all the clues you need to solve the mystery right along with hero Socrates Cheng.

What people are saying about
THE MOURNING WOMAN:

There are never enough five star mysteries out there for a dedicated reader like myself. Steven Roth has now written another in his Socrates Cheng private investigator series called, "The

Mourning Woman." His first was, "Mandarin Yellow," which I thought outstanding. Both have fascinating, complicated plots involving a mix of Chinese and Greek cultures. Roth's extensive credentials in the study of these groups has provided him with a unique perspective that fits perfectly with the genre of intrigue, historical vendetta, and motives unlikely to be uncovered easily by a typical American detective.

The Mourning Woman, the second in the series of Socrates Cheng mystery novels, is an intelligent and engrossing murder mystery that is stylish, well-crafted, and every bit as satisfying as Steven M. Roth's debut Cheng mystery, Mandarin Yellow. Roth is a great storyteller. I look forward to the third installment of the series.

What people are saying about
THE COUNTERFEIT TWIN

Compelling, fast moving, suspenseful read. Iconic Confederate General Robert E. Lee's ancestry is central to this third novel in the Socrates Cheng series by rising author Steven M. Roth. You will be introduced to the world of Civil War reenactors, to a secretive Confederate museum that has been robbed of documents containing potentially explosive revelations, and to an accomplished, mysterious assassin for hire. All add up to a mystery that will keep you entertained and guessing until you have turned the final pages.

STEVEN M. ROTH

FLEEING THE DRAGON

FLEEING
THE
DRAGON

A Sun-Jin 1945 Shanghai Mystery

STEVEN M. ROTH

BLACKSTONE PRESS

A CRIME BOOK IMPRINT

MYSTERY AND SUSPENSE/THRILLER NOVELS BY STEVEN M. ROTH

Socrates Cheng Mystery Series:
MANDARIN YELLOW
THE MOURNING WOMAN
THE COUNTERFEIT TWIN

Trace Austin Suspense/Thriller Series:
NO SAFE PLACE
NO PLACE TO HIDE

1930s-1940s Shanghai Mystery Series:
DEATH IN THE FLOWERY KINGDOM
DEATH OF THE YELLOW SWAN
SLEEPING WITH THE TIGER
FLEEING THE DRAGON

Children's Mystery:
THE MYSTERY OF THE MISSING DONUT:
A Mystery Introducing Owen Roth, Boy Detective

Written with Owen M. Roth
THE DOG WHO PLAYED CENTERFIELD:
A Dog & Baseball Story

Published by Blackstone Press, a Crime Book imprint

Cover design by Streetlight Graphics, LLC

ISBN: 978-1-7328748-5-5

FIRST EDITION

Visit the author's website: www.StevenMRoth.com

For Dominica and Owen

"People who do not believe in dragons
often find themselves eaten by one."

Attributed to Lao Tzu

A NOTE ON SPELLING, DATES, ETC.

I have used the Wade-Giles romanization of Chinese proper names, provinces, rivers, creeks, towns, cities, and Chinese-language expressions throughout this novel because this was the transliteration method in use in the 1940s.

AUTHOR'S WARNING TO READERS

This novel, by some current Western standards, is neither politically correct nor woke.

The story takes place in Shanghai in the 1940s when the Chinese Communist Party [CCP] and the People's Liberation Army defeated Chiang Kai-shek's Nationalist Kuomintang government and its Nationalist army [KMT], driving them from mainland China to the island of Taiwan. Many of the customs, statements, attitudes, and outlooks prevalent in China at that time not only might be alien to what we believe or accept in the twenty-first century in this country, but also might be offensive to some people if portrayed in a novel set in the present day.

Since FLEEING THE DRAGON is a 1940s novel, I have tried to reflect the lives, language, and attitudes of the Western Shanghailander expatriates and the indigenous Chinese Shanghainese people as they existed then, based on my research into then-contemporary English-language newspapers and magazines published in Shanghai, and also as reflected in many

English-language personal journals published after the Second World War and after the Chinese Civil War. In doing so, I have deliberately not considered twenty-first century language, customs or sensibilities in writing this story. I have used the slang and terminology of then-contemporary Shanghai, and have tried to reflect the attitudes and mores existing in Shanghai in the 1940s even though these might jar current sensibilities.

If this might bother you, I suggest you not read this book.

A Glossary of terms and phrases used in this book appears after the story.

PART ONE

JUNE 1945

CHAPTER 1

Sun-jin

Fourth week of June. Shanghai.

I WAS SITTING IN MY OFFICE at Blue Dragon Detective Agency in Shanghai's former International Settlement when suddenly the door flew open, slamming against the wall.

I leaped up and, as I did so, opened the top drawer of my desk and grabbed my revolver. I took aim at the open doorway.

Three soldiers rushed in.

"*Ayeeyah!* — *Damn!*" I shouted, taking aim at the closest man. "Who are you? What the hell is going—"

These soldiers, like me, were Chinese — were Celestials — not Kwantung Dwarf Bandits as I instinctively expected them to be under the Occupation. Yet these Celestials wore the uniform of the enemy army.

Are these Celestials collaborators who aid our enemy? I wondered. *Are they here to arrest me and put me into one of their internment camps as they did a few years ago?*

These questions cascaded through my mind in a split second.

"Put down your gun," one of the men shouted at me,

pointing his finger at my weapon. He spoke Mandarin to me, the language of educated Celestials.

Who were these men? I wondered.

The other two soldiers spread apart, standing on either side of me, and pointed their rifles at me.

I reluctantly complied with the order and raised my hands above my head.

The man who shouted at me stepped over to the desk, picked up the revolver, and placed it on a table, far out of my reach. Then he stepped back. The other men kept me covered.

"Are you Ling Sun-jin?" he said.

"*Shi — Yes.* I'm Sun-jin. What's going on?" I spoke to him in Mandarin, trying to steady my voice. I did not want to reveal my fear. My legs suddenly felt unsteady.

"You will come with us."

I was being arrested after all! I thought.

The spokesman stepped closer to me.

"Turn around so your back faces me," he said. "Hold your arms out from your sides."

He patted me down. Based on his skill searching me for a hidden weapon, I suspected that he, like me, was a former Shanghai Municipal policeman, but probably, unlike me, was not a disgraced, justifiably fired, former policeman.

"Am I under arrest?" I said. "Who are you? Why do you wear the uniform of our country's enemy?"

"You will come with us now." He pointed to the office door, directing me to walk there. "Come now!" he said, his voice becoming louder and more belligerent. "We have no time to waste."

What does he mean, we have no time to waste? Why not? I wondered.

Although these men had not threatened to harm me, I was worried about my safety, concerned about leaving the office with them. Who knew where they planned to take me or what they planned to do to me when we arrived there. This whole scenario had the feeling of an emerging kidnapping, a frequent problem in Japanese-occupied Shanghai.

I had been holding my arms above my head this whole time, but now I slowly lowered them to my sides, being sure to keep my hands in plain sight. I faced the man who had spoken to me, the soldier who had checked me for weapons. I assumed he was the leader.

"I would like to call my wife," I said to him. "She will be worried if I do not come home at my usual time."

"That's not possible," he answered, shaking his head as he turned me down. "There's no time to waste."

Strange, I thought. *There was that statement again.*

I had no choice but to follow his orders. I nodded, looked at the leader, and said to him, "*Maskee – No problem.* Let's go."

I walked out of my office. The three soldiers followed me.

I had no idea what I might be walking into.

We walked down four flights of stairs — the building's lift had been out of order for the past eleven months because there were no replacement parts available to maintain or repair it.

We exited the office building. I looked around, expecting to see more soldiers. We were alone.

One of the men escorting me pointed toward the curb directly in front of us.

"You walk there," he said, speaking to me in Hu, the street

language of Shanghai. I've spoken Hu and understood it all my life since I grew up in the city.

I started walking. The three Celestials followed me.

We headed toward the curb where a long, black 1938 Buick touring-style automobile was parked. The car's engine was running. I noticed that the car's small rear window on the passenger's side, along the curb facing us, was covered with a blackout curtain. No one could see into the car. This worried me. It suggested I was being kidnapped after all.

As we approached the car, its back door opened and a Celestial stepped out. He stood behind the door and held it open for me. He, too, wore the uniform of the enemy Kwantung.

Another collaborator, another traitor? I thought.

As we approached him, the man said to me, also speaking Hu, "Get in. Don't try no funny business. I'm watching you." He eyed me suspiciously.

Were all these Celestials just pretending to be Dwarf-Bandit soldiers or were they traitors, collaborating with the enemy? What were Celestial soldiers doing in occupied Shanghai?

I climbed into the back of the car, took one of the two jump seats facing toward the front, and sat quietly. I placed my hands on my lap, plainly in sight. I remained silent, waiting for instructions. Sweat pooled under my arms.

The man who had held the door open for me took the front passenger seat alongside the driver. The other three men filled the remaining jump seats, one sitting alongside me, facing the driver's back. The other two men sat facing us, our knees almost touching. To attempt to escape from the car — if I were even inclined to be so foolish — would require that I somehow scramble over their knees and laps and out the locked rear door. I had no intention of trying that.

I still had hope, as naïve as that now seems to me, that I would return home today in time for supper with my wife and children. I hoped that this was a case of mistaken identity, that these men really were looking for someone else even though they had specifically asked me my name after they burst into my office.

No one spoke as we sat there, the car's engine still idling.

After a few minutes, another car pulled up alongside us. I would later notice, when we reached our destination and I had climbed out of the Buick, that this other car had the Kwantung army's insignia painted on both its front doors. I also noticed that the men inside that other car were actual Dwarf Bandits, not, as in my car, Celestials dressed as if they were Dwarf-Bandit soldiers.

Our driver rolled down his window and spoke to someone in the other car. Although I could not see that other person because of the blackout curtain blocking the small window next to me, I could plainly hear him as if he was speaking to me. He, too, spoke the vernacular Hu, but with a pronounced Dwarf-Bandit accent.

My attention was caught by what the man in the other car said.

I knew now I would not be seeing my wife, Mei-hua, or our twins tonight. Perhaps not ever again.

I began to tremble.

CHAPTER 2

Soong Mei-ling (Madam Chiang Kai-shek)

One week earlier. Third week of June. Chungking and Shanghai.

SOONG MEI-LING, OFTEN REFERRED TO as the Dragon Lady — but only behind her back — was better known throughout Unoccupied China and in the West as Madam Chiang, the wife of Chiang Kai-shek, the Nationalist government's president and the leader of the KMT army. She was her husband's closest advisor and his most trusted confidant. Perhaps, some said, his only trusted advisor and confidant, but they would be wrong about that. Madam Chiang's older brother also occasionally filled these roles for Generalissimo Chiang.

Madam Chiang was a daughter of privilege, the fourth youngest of the six children of Charlie Soong, one of China's wealthiest men until his mysterious death by poisoning in 1918.

She had two older sisters — Soong Ching-ling and Soong Al-ling. She had one older brother, Soong Tse-ven (known as, T.V.), and two younger brothers, Soong T.A. and Soong T.L.

Madam Chiang was a woman infused with physical beauty. She oozed instinctive charm and much culture. She blended Eastern traditions with Western learning, having been educated in the United States, first at a Methodist middle school in

Macon, Georgia, then at Wellesley College in Massachusetts. She spoke fluent English with a slight Georgia lilt.

Madam Chiang also was a women steeped in the frailties of human nature, especially when it came to men. She was not beyond using her beauty and her learned charm to manipulate men, especially men in power who could aid her husband.

When in 1936 a rogue warlord kidnapped Generalissimo Chiang in the province of Xi'an — a warlord who believed Chiang's KMT should stop fighting Mao Tse-tung and the CCP, and instead should concentrate its limited resources resisting Japanese aggression in China — Madam Chiang, along with T.V., negotiated Chiang's release. They also negotiated a temporary truce — called the Xi'an Agreement — between Chiang and Mao, between the KMT and the CCP.

As part of the Xi'an Agreement, Chiang and Mao had carved out territories in China over which each would hold exclusive sway. Both men agreed not to fight the other until the undeclared war with Japan had been won. The anomalous truce worked for the most part, with only occasional fighting occurring between Mao's and Chiang's forces when they chanced upon one another in the far western provinces of China where the Japanese never strayed.

During the War Against Japanese Aggression — as the Chinese referred to the Second World War — Madam Chiang turned on her charm to win popular support for China among the American public. She wrote many articles for popular American magazines (especially for Henry Luce's *Time* and *Life* magazines, as well as for Luce's rivals' magazines, *Cosmopolitan* and the *Saturday Evening Post*). She also wrote feature articles for several prominent American newspapers, especially for the well-respected *New York Times*.

All the articles she wrote glorified a fanciful China in the imagined image portrayed in Pearl Buck's 1931 fiction best seller, THE GOOD EARTH. And all Madam Chiang's published writings, directly or subtly, urged America to aid China in its fight against the Japanese by sending China money, weapons, and supplies.

It was the easy availability of this aid, most of which was diverted by Chiang from the war effort to his personal use, that earned the physically diminutive Chiang Kai-shek his nickname in the West — the Little Bandit.

In February 1943, Madam Chiang toured the United States. While there, she addressed, charmed, and seduced a joint session of Congress. After that, money and armaments steadily flowed into China like the oncoming waters of a storm-glutted river.

In the third week of June, Madam Chiang secretly arrived in Japanese-occupied Shanghai. She went directly to the Cathay Hotel in the International Settlement. There she clandestinely met with representatives of the Japanese diplomatic service who had come from Tokyo to Shanghai expressly for the meeting.

Madam Chiang was there on behalf of her husband who wanted to negotiate a secret truce with the Kwantung army. Chiang intended to stop fighting the Japanese, to unilaterally and secretly tear-up the Xi'an Agreement he had entered into with Mao, and to turn all his attention to destroying Mao and the CCP. Under the secret treaty, Chiang's KMT army and the Japanese Kwantung would, for now, ignore each other.

It was Chiang's expectation that with his KMT army fighting Mao at the same time the Japanese Kwantung also would be engaged against Mao, the CCP soon would be defeated and Mao's power destroyed. Chiang then would turn his attention to driving the Kwantung from China, achieving two of his principal goals — Mao's defeat and ridding China of the Japanese.

Several members of Chiang's general staff disagreed with this strategy. They opposed his plan.

One group thought the plan was foolish, that Chiang's army could not defeat the Japanese without Mao's help, that Chiang was bound to fail, and that, as a result, China would be destroyed by the Kwantung. They urged Chiang not to pursue his plan.

One general said, "Without Mao, we will be hopelessly outnumbered. We cannot possibly be victorious over the Dwarf Bandits."

"Not so," said Chiang. "Now that the Germans have surrendered to the Round-Eyes, and the war is over in Europe, the Americans and British will step up their efforts in China to defeat the Dwarf Bandits. They will send us more money and more weapons, as well as their own troops, to use to defeat their enemy here. We will not be alone in our fight against the Kwantung.

"As the Round-Eyes fight the Dwarf Bandits here, we will pay lip-service to aiding them, but will use our new financial aid and weapons resources we receive from the Americans to finally defeat Mao so he will not rise again," he said.

Another general said, "Why would the Dwarf Bandits even be willing to agree to a truce with us? So far, they have had us on the defensive, even with Mao's army assisting us. I think your idea, Generalissimo, is preposterous."

Chiang stood up from behind his desk and paced the room. He drew heavily on his cigarette. His anger became apparent as his pace quickened and his face darkened. He confronted his generals head on.

"The Allies have the Dwarf Bandits on the run throughout the Pacific region. Only the foolish among the Kwantung would not see the advantage of entering into a truce with us so they can free up their troops and materials in China to be used elsewhere against the Round-Eyes.

"The Dwarf Bandits are so full of arrogance that they still believe they ultimately will defeat the Allies, and that their present, hopeless situation is merely a temporary setback.

I have no doubt," Chiang said, "that they foolishly believe that after they have defeated the Round-Eyes, they will be able to turn their attention back to us and will be able to conquer all of China."

Other members of Chiang's general staff found Chiang's idea unpatriotic, even traitorous. They believed it was Chiang's primary obligation to stand by his Xi'an Agreement with Mao, and, with the Communists' assistance, to drive the Dwarf Bandits into the sea.

Chiang ignored his generals' advice and sent his wife to Shanghai to meet with the Japanese diplomats to negotiate the truce with them.

The generals were not happy, but they mostly kept their objections to themselves. Those few who did not show this discretion quietly disappeared.

When the Kwantung agreed to enter into a secret truce with Chiang, several high-ranking Kwantung officers entertained a similar view of the situation as had Chiang's dissenting generals. In their case, however, the Code of the Bushido — a warrior's code of strict obedience to authority — prevented them from making their dissents known. They kept their objections to themselves.

The prevailing view in Tokyo was almost the mirror image of Chiang's perception. The detached, ruling Japanese believed they could stop fighting Chiang for now, allow the KMT and the CCP to weaken each other as they fought against each other for the supremacy of China, and that after one Chinese army had defeated the other — the Kwantung did not care which one prevailed — and after the Kwantung defeated the Allies, that they would then destroy the weakened Chinese victor — Chiang or Mao — and would subdue all of China.

In Shanghai, Madam Chiang negotiated and signed the secret truce on behalf of her husband, packed her valise with signed counterparts of the brief document, and left the Cathay Hotel to return to the airport for her flight back to Chungking.

With luck and a favorable tail wind, she thought, *I will be back with my husband in Chungking, with the signed treaty in my hand, in about six or seven hours.*

CHAPTER 3

Sun-jin

Current week. Fourth week of June. Shanghai.

L IFE HAS BEEN DIFFICULT IN *Shanghai since the Dwarf Bandits took over the International Settlement,* I thought.

Our city was in its eighth year of war against Japan. The first four years (from July 1937) were part of the undeclared, but very real, Second Sino-Japanese War. The most recent three years of this war were part of the broader Second World War involving both the British and the American Round-Eyes, among other Western countries.

The International Settlement ended abruptly as a Western treaty-port concession occupied and controlled by British and American Round-Eyes when Kwantung troops stormed into the treaty port on December 8, 1941. This occurred immediately after the Japanese attacked the American base at Pearl Harbor, Territory of Hawaii. The few Round-Eyes troops then in Shanghai, and all the Western diplomats and businessmen, as well as their families in the International Settlement, were taken by surprise and surrendered without a shot being fired on either side.

By the end of 1941, all Shanghai, including the French

Concession (which Japan had originally avoided occupying as a favor to its Axis ally, Vichy France) was fully occupied by the Kwantung.

Life for the British, American, and other western military personnel and civilian Allied nationals swiftly and drastically changed. All Allied nationals aged fourteen years and older were required to report to Hamilton House near the Bund — that mile-long curve of eloquent waterfront — to register with the Japanese police and to receive photo-ID cards. The Westerners also received red armbands they were required to always wear when in public.

The Kwantung froze all bank accounts owned by Allied, expatriate nationals. They were allowed to withdraw only two thousand yuan each month, placing these once privileged and pampered foreign nationals at the city's poverty level.

Each day, the Kwantung issued new edicts that further restricted where Allied citizens could go within the city, what they were allowed to do, and how they conducted their lives. Most Allied nationals chose to remain in the relative safety of their homes.

In early 1942, the Dwarf Bandits issued the order that expatriate Round-Eyes had feared and had expected would come: all citizens of Allied countries were to be imprisoned. As a result, most Westerners were hastily loaded onto trucks and were sent to eight crowded and squalid, hastily erected, internment camps located in and around the outskirts of the city. We Celestials, however, if not individually considered to be dangerous to the Dwarf Bandits, or if not openly political, were not automatically interned. Since I was a mere, struggling, non-political PI, I was left alone for the time being. Later, for reasons related to an investigation I conducted, I would be sent to an internment camp for several days. It was not an experience I would like to repeat.

Like most indigenous Shanghainese — we Celestials — I found life difficult under the Occupation, as we locals called the Dwarf Bandits' presence in the city.

The Dwarf Bandits gradually tightened their control over all occupants of Shanghai, Celestials and Occidentals alike. Spies were everywhere. They were encouraged to report on everyone. Every neighborhood had its watchdog spy — these were Celestials — who reported to the Dwarf Bandits. Waiters and servants were ordered to report on people in their establishments and households.

Everyone had to register births, deaths, overnight guests, and family members who had gone away from the household and city. It was increasingly difficult to hide from the watchful eyes of the enemy Dwarf Bandits.

We were required to register everyone in our household, and we each were given a photo-ID-card which we had to produce on demand by any Dwarf Bandit. To encourage everyone to register, food-ration coupons for rice, cooking oil, and other essentials were distributed only when we showed our ID cards. No one in a household was entitled to receive rationing coupons if anyone in that household had not registered.

Everyone was hungry. All the time. There was little food

available for civilians because the Kwantung confiscated almost all of it to feed its troops.

The Kwantung did not pay for what it took from farmers and merchants. This discouraged farmers from growing food or from raising livestock or poultry. It also discouraged merchants from setting up their booths because often the merchants had little or no food nor other merchandise to sell. Even the unlawful black market became too expensive for most of us to rely on.

This severe food shortage triggered a major riot that occurred during a soccer game at the Canidrome, the large entertainment complex with its sports arena, dog racetrack, and giant ballroom. But the food riot brought no relief. Worse, it brought retribution from the Dwarf Bandits. As punishment, the Japanese navy blockaded Shanghai, preventing the city from receiving any shipments of rice and other supplies. At markets, after the imposition of the blockade, people often stood waiting in line with their ration coupons long before dawn, only to eventually find out that rice and other staples were not available. By 1944, the Japanese's depleted war machine was bearing down on civilians more severely than ever to squeeze out critical resources.

People were persistently ill. Often, very ill. Disease and resulting sickness were prevalent, probably as a result of malnutrition. Medicine was scarce because such little medicine as did become available from time to time was confiscated by the Kwantung for use by its troops. Deaths among civilians increased dramatically over the number of deaths from illnesses and natural causes that occurred before the Occupation.

All in all, we were a city forced to bend to the ill will and to the occasional largess of the occupying enemy. This showed on every street corner — on corners where the Kwantung maintained machine-gun nests; in every struggling business or abandoned merchant's stall; and, in every civilian's home, many of whom were forced to house Kwantung soldiers at the expense of the families living there.

It was an ill-advised time to be a Shanghainese, I thought.

CHAPTER 4

Sun-jin

Current week. Fourth week of June. Shanghai.

SHOULD INTRODUCE MYSELF.

My name is Ling Sun-jin. I am 44 years old and married to Wu Mei-hua. We have twin children – a boy and a girl. They are four years old under our Celestial calendar which, as everyone knows, counts the day of birth as year one; they are three years old under the West's Round-Eyes' calendar. Our daughter was born first. Our son closely followed her. Our daughter's name is Ling Fen. Our son's name is Ling Ji. Fen and Ji.

Our twins have very different personalities. Fen's personality mirrors her mother's. Like Mei-hua, our daughter is a revolutionary at heart. Well, in young Fen's case, she as yet is only a revolutionary in the making. She is confident, assertive, and very strong-willed. She seems to take delight in defying our authority. Fen's favorite word when we instruct her to do something is *Bú – No*. She rarely smiles and always seems suspicious of her circumstances. She bosses her twin brother as if she is an adult and he is the child in the family. She frequently snatches his toys from his hands and runs off with them, laughing as she does so. She tends to stare at me or Mei-hua as she runs off smiling, as if challenging us to discipline her. We rarely do so, a trait common among the parents of Celestial children.

Our son's personality is very different from Fen's. Ji is quiet, retiring, introspective, anxious to please his elders, and prefers to be told what he should or should not do. He then seems comfortable conforming to what he's been told. Ji will become a fine Confucian when he is older. His innate nature is there already.

I should mention, too, that Mei-hua and I have a third child — well, we call her that even though she is not really our child, but she certainly is a member of our family. This so-called third child is our *huang gou* — our *wild dog*. Her name is *Bik — Jade*. Bik has been part of our lives since the day Mei-hua and I met. Over the years, in the course of my private investigation business, Bik has saved my life on at least three occasions I can think of. She has twice saved Mei-hua's life.

Bik is an integral part of our family. Wisely, she seems wary of Fen, but comfortable with Ji. For a stray mutt I fortuitously acquired in the woods about ten years ago, Bik is no fool.

Now, more about me.

For many years, until 1937, I was a Shanghai Municipal Police inspector-detective. Specifically, I worked as part of the elite Special Branch, having an excellent arrest and crime-solving record, making a good living. I was abruptly fired from that lofty position when I deliberately disobeyed my superior's order during an investigation involving one of the International Settlement's most wealthy and powerful men — Victor Sassoon. Since then, I have had no choice but to work unlawfully as an unlicensed private investigator, carrying an unlicensed gun, and always, therefore, operating outside the law. I am at constant risk of being arrested and sent to prison by the authorities for want of a detective's license and a weapon permit.

From 1937 until the Occupation in December 1941, my PI business steadily grew. My principal clients were Chinese businessmen and merchants, as well as criminal triads and their members. I also represented many Jewish immigrants who had fled the Nazis and had settled in the Jewish section of Hongkew. I occasionally also helped White Russian immigrants who had fled the Communist revolution in Russia in 1917. Because I am Celestial, neither the British nor the American Round-Eyes living in Shanghai ever gave me any of their business. The Jewish community, on the other hand, has been generous with me and, until the Occupation, kept me very busy because I had been befriended by one of that community's leaders, a man named Avram Ben-David Reuben.

Once the Dwarf Bandits took over our city in 1941, and imposed travel, commerce, and very strict curfew limitations on Shanghai's inhabitants and businesses, my number of clients, and the number of cases for me to investigate, rapidly declined. Since then, I have struggled to make a sustainable living for my family.

CHAPTER 5

Madam Chiang

One week earlier. Third week of June. Shanghai.

MADAM CHIANG WAS PLEASED WITH the results she achieved when she met with the Dwarf-Bandit diplomats to negotiate her husband's secret treaty. She was especially pleased with herself for having been the person who had obtained those results.

She had accomplished everything her husband wanted without conceding anything he was not prepared to give up. The Japanese agreed to end all fighting against the KMT and to increase the frequency and ferocity of their combat against Mao's CCP, especially in the central highlands where Chiang's KMT forces were sparce, but Mao's forces were strong. Her husband would be pleased when he saw the results of her efforts.

Madam Chiang entered the third car in a five-vehicle secret convoy that would swiftly take her to an airport located outside Shanghai, just three kilometers from the Cathay Hotel where the meeting and negotiations had taken place. There she would board the same Chinese National Aviation Corporation's Douglas DC-3 that had flown her from Chungking to Shanghai. With luck and with a strong tailwind, she soon would be back in China's wartime capital and then in Chiang's skinny, but strong arms.

The ride to the airport was going quickly. Madam Chiang closed her eyes and briefly napped, taking advantage of the blackout curtains covering the rear-side windows of the car, partially blocking out the afternoon sunlight.

She abruptly awoke to the sound of the soldier in the front-passenger's seat suddenly shouting *"Hai!"* and to the violent swaying motion of the car as it sharply braked, fish-tailed, then skidded. She was thrown against the back side of the passenger's front seat, then against the rear side-door's window, bruising her forehead.

She barely had time to consider what had happened when the unmarked civilian car immediately in front of her car responded to a nearby explosion and banked sharply right, veering off the road. The car rolled over and over on its sides, finally coming to a halt, resting upside down on its crushed roof. Smoke poured out from under its hood.

Ayeeyah! My assistants are in that car! she thought.

She turned around to look at the overturned car through the back window, and watched as her vehicle accelerated, speeding away from the volatile scene and away from the contorted, burning car that moments before had been on its way with them to the airport.

Madam Chiang watched as the soldier in the front seat of her car rolled down his window and poked his head out, looking behind them as they sped away.

She leaned forward toward the driver. She placed her hand lightly on his shoulder, and spoke softly, speaking Mandarin, the only Chinese dialect she knew, her voice conspicuously controlled.

"Stop," she said, "Turn the car around. We must go back. My assistants are in that burning car."

The driver, a Kwantung soldier who spoke no Chinese, let alone the Mandarin dialect of the educated, ignored her, shaking his shoulder free, making it clear he wanted her to remove her hand. He said nothing.

The other soldier turned to face Madam Chiang. He shouted, speaking heavily-accented Hu. "We were ambushed. Hold onto something. This ride is going to be rough. We will be at the airport in a few minutes."

Madam Chiang had no idea what he had said.

CHAPTER 6

T.V. Soong

Current week. Fourth week of June. Chungking.

T.V. Soong was Madam Chiang's favorite brother among her three male siblings. It was T.V. she called upon in 1936 to help her negotiate the release of Chiang from the warlord. It had required a carriage full of gold, not politics, paid to the warlord by T.V. from his own funds that convinced the kidnapper to set Chiang free.

T.V., in turn, was devoted to his sister. At her urging, since he was a capitalist at heart and had seen his role during China's period of recent strife as that of amassing a personal fortune, he reluctantly gave up that endeavor and accepted the office of Finance Minister for the KMT. He entered Chiang's government in that capacity.

T.V. was a financial genius. He successfully brought China's hyper-inflation under control. To achieve this, he strong-armed Nationalist banks from time-to-time to make large, low-interest loans to the government, such loans secured only by questionable bonds repeatedly issued by that same, borrowing government, for that very same purpose. The proceeds of the loans mostly found their way into Chiang's off-shore bank accounts. T.V. never enriched himself that way. He was a facilitator and a patriot, not a thief.

CHAPTER 7

Big-Eared Tu

Current week. Fourth Week of June. Chungking.

BIG-EARED TU WAS ONE OF the wealthiest and most powerful men in China, all the result of the many criminal enterprises he had conducted since the late 1920s, as the leader of Shanghai's notorious Green Gang triad.

When the Japanese took control of Shanghai in 1941, it made no difference to Big-Eared Tu. He merely left the city and moved his headquarters to Chungking, following Chiang's example. He continued to control all organized crime he had left behind in Shanghai.

It was said that Tu had an army of paid informants everywhere — Celestials who acted as his eyes and ears, men and women who haunted the teahouses, gambling dens, opium emporiums, and other places prohibited to foreigners — and that, as a result, he knew everything significant that went on in China. This generally was true. He certainly knew what went on in Shanghai, although he hadn't set foot there in four years.

Although he was a major criminal, Tu liked to present himself as a benevolent, kind old man — a charitable man, a community-minded citizen. He was anything but that.

Big-Eared Tu controlled the vast opium and heroin trades, the flower-seller girls prostitution business, all gambling clubs, the protection and extortion rackets, Shanghai's trade unions, and the French Concession's police — having arranged for his Green Gang deputy, Pock-Marked Huang, to be Frenchtown's chief of police.

To advance the benign image of himself he liked to project, Tu sat on the boards of directors of several legitimate banks, schools, fraternal organizations, and charities. This fooled no adult who had been awake in Shanghai for any part of the past twenty years. Everyone knew that Tu, who always spoke softly — especially when he was angry — was not the kind, elderly citizen he pretended to be or, at least, not the elderly citizen of Shanghai he strove to project himself as being.

Nor was he the wise, old philanthropist he sometime pretended to be — although he did distribute a great deal of cash in Shanghai. But this *squeeze* — *bribes* — was not doled out to help charities and the city's poor. It was dispensed to assist Tu in furthering his criminal enterprises.

Tu had a cruel side, too. In 1938, when he learned that two rival triad leaders had spoken ill of him in public, causing him to lose face, Tu invited both men to his home for a banquet, the stated purpose of which was to talk through their rivalries and to make peace with one another.

Acting on Tu's orders, his chef intentionally laced the meal with poison. Tu made an excuse not to eat it. One guest died in agony that evening; the other barely survived after being violently ill for weeks. Tu, impervious to the possibility of punishment for his action, spread the word he had deliberately poisoned his rivals because they had mocked him.

On another occasion, a stockbroker, hoping to endear

himself with the city's leading criminal, gave Tu a stock tip based on secret information he'd obtained. Tu invested heavily in the stock, giving the young broker $20,000-face-value of highly-depreciated Chinese yuan. Within three weeks the stock had become worthless.

Tu's men brought the hapless stockbroker to Tu's office at the Collective Prosperity Club. He'd been bound hand and foot and had been beaten by his captors. Tu gave the man two choices: do nothing and have his throat cut within one hour; or, return within one hour and give Tu a gift of $40,000 value in gold bars to make up for the man's transgression. The stockbroker chose the latter path, and left with one of Tu's men to round up the gold. Upon returning home, the man later told his employer, he found an empty coffin sitting on the floor next to his bed. He took this as a warning from Tu to leave the stock business altogether. The man resigned his position the next morning and left Shanghai.

CHAPTER 8

Eli

Two weeks earlier. Second week of June. Shanghai.

ELI BEN-DAVID REUBEN HAD ADJUSTED well to life under the Occupation. This was not surprising. After all, the Occupation was just an extension of the severe adjustment he'd been forced to make when he and his family fled the Nazis in 1935, left their home in Breslau, Germany, and emigrated to Shanghai as stateless immigrants.

Much good luck — what the Chinese call good *joss* — had been involved in easing his transition from life before the Occupation to life under the Occupation.

It had been lucky, for example, that Eli's father had once hired Sun-jin to investigate the theft of a valuable postage stamp stolen from his store's philatelic inventory. It had been good *joss*, too, that Sun-jin had been successful in recovering the stamp and in bringing the thief to justice. It also had been lucky that Sun-jin and Eli's father had then become close friends, and that Eli's father had once suggested to him that he ask Sun-jin if he would teach Eli to become a private investigator. And it had been good *joss* that Sun-jin had agreed to do so, and that, as a result, Eli had resigned his dangerous position as editor of the CCP's underground newspaper, *Slovo — the Word*.

That had been just over four years ago. Now, Eli was fairly seasoned as a PI, and he had become a contributing asset to Sun-jin and to his struggling PI business.

Eli was at home when Sun-jin telephoned him.

"We need to meet this morning," Sun-jin said. "Something's come up."

"I plan to come in about 10:00 a.m. Will that be all right?"

"*Ayeeyah!* I suppose. It's important. Don't be late."

"Is there a problem?"

"Just come in to meet," Sun-jin said.

"What's the problem?" Eli asked, as he stepped into Sun-jin's office. "This mystery approach to a conversation isn't like you."

"Sit," Sun-jin said, as he pointed to a chair near his desk.

Sun-jin paused. "This is difficult for me to say." He looked hard at Eli. "I have no choice." He felt his back stiffen.

"Have I done something wrong?" Eli asked.

Sun-jin shook his head. "*Bú — No*. You haven't done anything wrong, but there is something wrong."

He paused, took a deep breath, slowly let it out, then said, "I can't afford to keep you on Blue Dragon's payroll. You know how little business we have these days. I have to let you go."

Eli laughed, then quieted down and grinned. He slowly shook his head. "*Oy veh!* Is that what this is about? That's not a problem. I'll just stay and work without pay."

He smiled and nodded several times as if confirming that he'd actually heard himself say that.

"I can't let you do that," Sun-jin said. "It's a matter of pride for me. I should have been able to make this business succeed, even under the Occupation and working unlawfully in the shadows. I can't allow you to work for free."

"Of course you can, Boss," Eli said. His face became serious. "What other job can I find under the Occupation? Does anyone need the services of the former editor of the enemy-Communist's newspaper or the services of a partially trained PI? I doubt it."

"There are other PI firms that—"

Eli held up his palm to quiet Sun-jin, a rare showing of disrespect for him.

"Will any of our competitors hire me? I don't think so. Their business situation shouldn't be any different than ours."

Sun-jin nodded, but said nothing.

"So, if I am going to go broke and starve, I would just as soon continue to work for you without pay. I can starve here at the office as well as I can sitting alone at home. In the meantime, I'll learn more about the business from you. That will help us when this war finally is over and the Japs are gone."

Sun-jin started to say something, hesitated, then smiled. He reached out to shake Eli's hand.

"In that case," he said, "why don't you become my partner?"

Eli smiled. "Are you serious?"

"From this moment on, Eli, you own twenty-five percent of Blue Dragon. That gives you, at the moment, twenty-five percent of almost nothing. … Well, actually, it gives you twenty-five percent of nothing. Except for the used furniture, which is practically worthless, we have no assets. Welcome to the business, Partner."

CHAPTER 9

Mei-hua

Current week. Fourth week in June. Shanghai.

MEI-HUA CELEBRATED HER THIRTY-SIXTH BIRTHDAY this week. She was a very different woman than she'd been in 1937 when she first met Sun-jin on the lawn outside *Wing On* department store in the International Settlement.

Long before that day, for many years before she met Sun-jin, Mei-hua had been an ardent Communist and an active revolutionary. She'd been a sworn and vocal enemy of Chiang Kai-shek and of the Nationalist government, and was an outspoken admirer of Mao Tse-tung. She had even accompanied Mao on the Long March, although, to her regret, she had been forced to return home to Shanghai before the march reached its destination, when she fell ill from malnutrition and fatigue.

Afterward, as she slowly recuperated at her parents' home, she publicly renounced Mao, left the CCP, and took a mid-level, non-political job with the Nationalist government's Ministry of Justice. All this at the insistent urging of her KMT-colonel father who insisted that her affiliation with Mao and the CCP had hurt his army career. Life became routine and monotonous for her.

By 1937, the year she met Sun-jin, gone were the days when, as an ardent revolutionary, she had openly waged written and vocal war on opium, on concubinage, and on the old, decadent Confucian ideas that equated old age with wisdom or that associated someone's calligraphy skills with scholarship.

Mei-hua eventually became the housewife she is today, a woman who outwardly seemed content to stay at home in occupied Shanghai, a woman seemingly content to raise her two children. Yet she refused to commit fully. Unlike most married women in Nationalist China, Mei-hua had refused to take her husband's last name (Ling). Instead she retained her own last name (Wu). She remained, Wu Mei-hua.

The one other vestige of her former days as an aspiring revolutionary was her continued study and practice of the martial art known as *Shaolin*. Along with Sun-jin, who also had been a student of this martial art form before he and Mei-hua met, she spent at least two hours every morning practicing the form and sparring with her husband or with other students or instructors. Both Mei hua and Sun-jin were proficient in the form.

CHAPTER 10

Generalissimo Chiang Kai-shek

One week earlier. Third week of June. Chungking.

CHIANG PACED HIS OFFICE, CHAIN smoking, burning through two Yellow Tiger-brand cigarettes in less than fifteen minutes. His breathing was labored, quick and noisy. His shirt-back was wet from pooled sweat.

He abruptly stubbed out his cigarette in the heavy glass ashtray sitting on his desk, sending the ashtray over the edge and tumbling to the floor. Chiang ignored the mess he'd made on his carpet.

How dare they try to kill my wife. Don't those fools know who they are dealing with?

Whatever the answer to his rhetorical thought, Chiang knew that his plans to enter into the secret truce with the Dwarf Bandits had been aborted for the time being. The Dwarf Bandits had seen to that. They had contacted Chiang and called off the truce until they knew if the attack had been engineered by any of their officers who had silently opposed the agreement with Chiang.

Chiang, too, needed to know if his own officers had initiated the attack. Until he knew if the attempt to assassinate his wife was really the first step in a scheme to overthrow him as leader of the Nationalist government and the KMT army, he would keep close to the ground at headquarters.

Who can I trust to pursue this for me in enemy-occupied Shanghai? he wondered.

Who, indeed, could he trust?

Only a few members of his officer-staff had been with him from the beginning, from the 1920s. He barely trusted them, let alone those generals who were recent additions to his staff, necessitated by the uptick in the war. He certainly did not trust those few, surviving generals who had opposed his plan to enter into the temporary truce with the Dwarf Bandits, officers he was forced to keep alive because he needed their experience and skills for the prosecution of the war.

Who in occupied Shanghai, where the plot probably originated and was carried out, can I trust to discover the truth? he wondered.

He did not know the answer to this, but he knew who would know. He would visit his old friend, mentor, and fellow Green Gang member, Big-Eared Tu.

Tu would point Chiang in the right direction and would give him the name of a person still living in Shanghai who would help him.

Chiang called his driver to bring his car around front. As he stood to walk to the lift, to go to the ground floor, the office door opened. Madam Chiang walked in.

"Ah!" Chiang said. "Just the person I want to talk to. Sit down, my dear." He gestured toward the sofa and followed her across the room.

CHAPTER 11

Mei-hua and Sun-jin

Current week. Fourth week of June. Shanghai.

"WE NEED TO TALK," MEI-HUA said, as she and I sipped tea at our breakfast table.

"*Qing — Please*," I said. I wondered why Mei-hua seemed so serious this morning. So formal. "Are the twins all right? They seemed fine when I saw them a few minutes ago in their bedroom."

"It's not the children. It's me I want to talk about."

"*Shi — Yes.* I am always happy to talk about you." I bowed my head slightly, in respect, and smiled.

"I have given this matter much thought.". She stared into her teacup as she spoke. "I have decided Fen and Ji now are old enough that I can resume my former political activities and not cause them harm by my periodic absences from home."

"*Ayeeyah! — Damn!*" I said. I felt my face grow warm. I never expected that.

Mei-hua held up her palm to forestall my response. "Please listen to what I have to say, Sun-jin, before you offer your judgment."

I nodded and bowed my head again. "*Dúi bú qi — I'm sorry*. Please speak your piece."

"Now that the twins are age four, I feel I can safely leave them alone with an *amah*, and can rejoin the CCP to work with the Party to fight the Dwarf Bandits. It's my patriotic duty. I will stay in Shanghai, of course, but will participate underground with the CCP's resistance movement."

I was not happy to hear this, although it was not totally unexpected. Mei-hua had not been happy years ago when she had been forced by her father to sever her ties with the CCP. To satisfy him, she wrote a letter to the *North-China Daily News* in which she renounced the CCP and all it stood for, publicly ending her membership in the Party. I always knew she regretted doing that, and that she felt she'd had no choice.

"This could be very dangerous," I said. "It would be like climbing onto the back of an unruly dragon. Not only would you become an enemy of every Celestial in Unoccupied China, but also an enemy of the Dwarf Bandits in occupied China, specifically here at home in Shanghai where you are known.

"I know you miss the CCP, but to rejoin it, and especially to rejoin it with a view to participating in its Resistance movement against the Kwantung, and then to participate in the CCP's opposition to Chiang, as you inevitably would, might place our family in grave danger. Is that what you want?"

"Of course not. Don't even think that, Sun-jin."

"And yet that is exactly what you are planning on doing," I said.

Mei-hua took a deep breath. I could see I was causing her great frustration and anger. She pinched her lips together. Her nostrils flared.

"There will be constant danger for you, for all of us," I said, "even when you are not actively on a mission. There will always be informants who will be happy to turn you in to the Dwarf Bandits if it suits their desires. You cannot avoid that. Other people might report you to the KMT."

"I plan to be careful about which assignments I accept. The CCP has its own methods of rooting-out informants and of dealing with them. When I rejoin the CCP, I will use a *nom de guerre* so my true identity will not be known."

"You already are well known by sight," I said, "and, of course, because of your controversial renunciation letter to the newspaper. It is even possible there will be participants in the CCP's Resistance who resent your previous action and would be willing to turn you in to the Kwantung or to the KMT for that reason alone."

Mei-hua shrugged her shoulders. "I will be prudent. That's the best I can do. You need to trust me."

"Who will watch the children?" I asked.

"As I said, I will hire an *amah* I can trust. We will scrape by to pay her while your business is not doing well, but we'll be able to do it since the cost will be low. These days, even *amahs* cannot find work except for the odious families of the Dwarf Bandits, who treat the women as if they are slaves. Many *amahs* will be pleased to have the opportunity to work for a Celestial family, even for a low wage."

I sighed. I could see this was going nowhere. I had lost this battle.

"There's more," Mei-hua said. "I intend to invite Eli to join me again. He would be valuable to the cause if he agrees."

I was not happy, but I could see I would not be able to stop her, so I said, "I would like to talk more about this later.

I would like to think about it for a few days. Please don't say anything to Eli until we have spoken again about this."

Mei-hua rolled her eyes, but said nothing.

CHAPTER 12

Generalissimo Chiang Kai-shek

One week earlier. Third week of June. Chungking.

MADAM CHIANG'S UNPLANNED APPEARANCE IN Chiang's office gave rise to an argument that lasted more than forty minutes.

"*Qing — Please,* my wife," Chiang said, "you have it all wrong. I am not asking you to keep a low profile now that you have been a target of my enemies. I am ordering you to do so. You will obey me."

Madam Chiang crushed out her cigarette. Her eyes flashed. "No, you have it wrong, my husband. You do not give me orders. You make requests to me. Then I decide whether or not I will agree to do as you ask. I am not one of your flunky generals."

She stood to leave, and snatched her jeweled handbag from the nearby tabletop.

Chiang stood up. "Please, Mei-ling, do not leave. I have more to say. Please sit. I am worried about you."

Mei-ling shrugged one shoulder. "You always worry about me," she said. "My name is Beautiful Flower, not Delicate Flower. I will be fine."

She paused, then again took her former place on the sofa. She reached over and squeezed Chiang's hand. When she spoke again, she softened her tone.

"If I do not slink away and hide like some frightened schoolgirl, you will find I can be even more useful to you than I've been throughout our marriage. We can do this together if the occurrence of the plot against us is correctly managed."

Chiang sighed. "It will not be useful to me or to our cause if you are assassinated," he said. "I need you by my side as my wife and confidant — you, not my memory of you, not the nation's memory of you."

Mei-ling shook her head and put her hand gently on Chiang's arm. "My darling husband, the *fan kuei* — the *foreign devils, the* Round-Eyes, adore me — at least the Americans do — and that has directly benefited you and our cause beyond our wildest dreams.

"If I suddenly disappear from public view, what will the Americans think and how will they act? You know I am the key to their pocketbooks and weaponry."

Chiang remained silent, waiting to see where his shrewd wife would wander with this thought.

"Let us take advantage of the attack against me to stir up sympathy for me, and, as a result, sympathy for you. We should describe my near death to the editor of the *Chungking Daily*.

"We can say I was on a mission for you. No one has to know the nature of the mission or in which city the attempt on my life took place. The Americans, especially their foolish Congressmen and magazine editors, will revel in the story and in my close brush with death. It will enhance my image with them, as well as with our own public. And, you, my dear husband, will be the ultimate beneficiary of all that."

Chiang slowly shook his head and took both her hands in his.

"I intend to identify the traitor who tried to harm you," he said, "then execute him."

"*Hao — Good,*" Madam Chiang said. "When you do that, my darling, I will gladly be there to give the order to the hangman to pull the lever, or, perhaps, I will pull the lever myself."

CHAPTER 13

Eli and Mei-hua

Current week. Fourth week of June. Shanghai.

"Y OU'RE SERIOUS, MEI-HUA?" ELI SAID. He smiled. "You are recruiting me to rejoin the CCP and become active in its Resistance? Not just to edit *Slovo* again?"

"I'm serious, but we also will need you to publish and edit a Resistance newspaper. Nothing as elaborate as *Slovo*, but important nevertheless. A few pages distributed secretly from time to time to keep the faithful happy and advised."

"I'm anxious to join you," Eli said, "but before I can agree to do so I must speak with someone."

"Sun-jin?" Mei-hua said.

Eli nodded. "Of course. We now are more than friends and employer/employee. We now also are business partners in Blue Dragon."

"I'm sure Sun-jin will not be happy with your decision, or pleased that I've discussed this with you before he and I have talked more about my decision, but I don't think he will stand in your way."

Eli nodded. "Also, my father. I must speak with him. He, too, will not be happy, but he will respect my decision and will not block it."

CHAPTER 14

Chiang Kai-shek and Big-Eared Tu

One week earlier. Third week of June. Chungking.

AFTER HIS WIFE LEFT HIS office, Chiang, as he had started to do, visited Big-Eared Tu at Tu's wartime home located at No.888 Yellow Grasshopper Road.

They sat in Tu's Great Room among the few scholars' artifacts, calligraphy scrolls, watercolor paintings, and dynasty furniture that Tu had not hidden in a cave when he fled Shanghai for Chungking. Tu's songbirds and lucky crickets remained silent in their hanging cages while both men were present in the room.

Tu and Chiang had known and trusted each other since the late 1920s when Tu recruited Chiang to join the Green Gang triad. In return, Chiang, in the 1930s, when he gained power over the Republic and headed the Nationalist government, permitted Tu to continue to operate his opium business in Shanghai. Chiang did this even as he publicly, and with great fanfare, led several successful anti-opium campaigns against Tu's rivals. In return, Tu gave Chiang a significant portion of the income he earned from the opium business. This *squeeze* substantially funded Chiang's KMT army and his fight against Mao and the CCP.

After they exchanged the requisite Confucian and Taoist ritual greetings, Chiang said, "Mei-ling was almost assassinated last week while she was in Shanghai on a secret mission for me."

Tu, who was reputed to know everything important that occurred in Shanghai, frowned. *Why hadn't I already heard about this? I will have to deal with this problem as soon as Chiang leaves.*

Tu nodded. "*Shi — Yes.* I heard this had occurred. What was the nature of her mission?"

Chiang trusted Tu so he explained the mission he had sent his wife on. He described the ambush that occurred as she neared the airport for her flight back to Chungking.

Tu frowned. "Ah!" he said. "Have you asked yourself if the plot arose in Chungking among your generals or junior officers who secretly opposed the treaty?"

Chiang shrugged. "I am investigating that. It is too soon to know."

"The Dwarf Bandits must have known," Tu said. "Perhaps some Kwantung generals who opposed the treaty created the plot."

"I intend to investigate that aspect in Shanghai," Chiang said. "I want answers quickly so I can have the agreement reinstated. The Dwarf Bandits have suspended the truce until they know if their officers were involved. The truce is essential for our campaign against Mao."

"How do you propose to investigate this in an occupied city?" Tu said.

"That's why I am here, Master Tu. I would like you to suggest someone in Shanghai I can rely on, someone who has the skills and experience to investigate this crime. Someone who is discreet."

Tu nodded, but said nothing. He closed his eyes for a few seconds and thought about Chiang's request.

"I know such a person, but you will have to persuade him to help you. He is very stubborn and very independent."

"I can be persuasive," Chiang said.

"His name is Ling Sun-jin," Tu said. "He works as an unlicensed, illegal PI in Shanghai. His history suggests he is loyal to the KMT."

Chiang frowned. "I am familiar with his name, but I cannot recall why."

"He used to be a Special Branch inspector-detective with the municipal police. He was fired for insubordination. Then, after leaving the police, he was involved in the private investigation of the kidnapping of that famous Iraqi Jew, Victor Sassoon. He also investigated the death of the notorious nightclub singer, the young Dwarf-Bandit woman known as the Yellow Swan. Before all that, while he still was a cop, he investigated the murders of the flower-seller girls in the Flowery Kingdom.

"He has a long and distinguished record both on and off the Municipal Police force."

"Ah, yes. I recall him now." Chiang frowned again and shook his head. "Isn't his wife a Communist? Didn't she march with Mao before her father made her return to Shanghai and publicly renounce the CCP?"

"That's the woman," Tu said.

"Then how can we trust her husband?" Chiang said. "His wife might be a spy for the CCP. He also might be."

"I trust him," Tu said. "There were times when he could have lied to me, but did not. This was so even when lying to me would have benefited him or when telling me the truth, as he did, could have brought harm upon him."

Chiang shrugged. "And your advice, Master Tu?"

"I say, trust him, but have him closely watched. I can arrange that for you through our triad brethren still in Shanghai."

Chiang nodded as Tu stood up. The meeting was over.

CHAPTER 15

Big-Eared Tu

One week earlier. Third week of June. Chungking.

A s soon as Chiang left the Great Room, Tu rang a small bell that sat on a boxwood table beside him. The door opened and a servant entered carrying a tray containing a floral porcelain tea pot, two porcelain teacups, and two short-stem opium pipes.

At the same time, a curtain at the far end of the room parted and Pock-Marked Huang stepped out from behind it. Huang walked directly over to Tu. He seated himself on a silk pillow on the floor directly across from Tu, a rare *huanghuali*-wood table between them.

The men remained silent while the servant poured tea, retrieved a small vial of opium from an A-frame burlwood cabinet, then filled and lit their pipes for them.

As soon as they were alone, Tu said to Huang, "Chiang's plan, and his destructive treaty with the Dwarf Bandits, will not succeed. Chiang will never build his army sufficiently to defeat the Dwarf Bandits after they, together with Chiang, have defeated Mao and the CCP.

"Chiang is too greedy to use the military equipment and the

financial aid he will receive from the Round-Eyes to strengthen his army. The generalissimo will bleed the aid dry, rerouting it into his personal bank accounts, leaving just enough money with the KMT to seem to the Round-Eyes that he is achieving their purpose, rather than just feeding Chiang's hunger for wealth and power."

"Should we intervene, Master Tu?" Huang asked.

"Chiang could defeat the CCP army if he would use the aid to build his own army, but we both know he will not do that. His army, at the present, is under-staffed, under-trained, and under-equipped. It has no will to fight the CCP or the Dwarf Bandits. This will not improve as Chiang diverts resources to his personal accounts."

"What should we do?" Huang said.

Tu raised his bowl to his lips, slurped his tea, then said, "I will tell you."

CHAPTER 16

Sun-jin

Current week. Fourth week of June. Shanghai and Chungking.

T HE MEN IN ENEMY-KWANTUNG UNIFORMS led me from the Buick, up a set of stairs, into an airplane. They seated me on a bench running most the length of the cabin. I was alone except for two armed Celestials who, unlike the men who brought me here, wore the uniform of the KMT, not the uniform of the enemy Dwarf Bandits. They would not answer me when I asked where we were going.

The flight was uneventful. Just very noisy, bone-chilling cold in the unheated plane, and very slow. The trip took about six hours. I had not been told why I was put aboard the plane, so the flight seemed to go on forever.

I no longer worried about my safety. If I were going to be harmed by the guards, they could have done so already. I did not need to be flown six hours to be harmed by them somewhere other than in Shanghai. As the flight progressed, I had been more bored, more physically cold and uncomfortable, and more curious about our destination and the reason for the flight than I was frightened.

When the plane landed, I was taken to an awaiting car.

We drove for about twenty minutes. Then, my escorts and I entered an office building. I did not recognize the city we drove through to get to the office building.

"Come," one of the soldiers from the plane said to me, speaking Hu, as we climbed out of the car. He beckoned me forward with his arm.

Two soldiers I hadn't seen before walked in front of me. The two from the plane walked directly behind me. We rode a lift to the fifth floor. There, the soldiers handed me off to another soldier wearing a KMT dress uniform. He led me to an office door, and knocked.

I immediately recognized the man sitting behind the desk. My back stiffened and my legs began to shake. I had seen his photograph many times in newspapers, on magazine covers, in newsreels at the movie theater, and, before the war, on political campaign posters. I was dumbfounded to be in his presence.

He did not rise to greet me and did not smile to welcome me as I was led to a chair in front of his desk.

"Sit," Generalissimo Chiang said. He pointed to the chair. He did not look up at me as he pointed.

I sat down and stared at Chiang Kai-shek. I said nothing. I felt sweat pooling in my armpits and in the small of my back.

Chiang looked up and frowned. "Ling Sun-jin, you know who I am," he said. "Therefore, you also must know I would not waste my time bringing you here from Shanghai unless your presence is important to me."

I nodded. "Yes, sir."

"Are you a patriot, Mr. Ling?"

I noticed his voice was high-pitched, almost squeaky. That

surprised me. I had never heard him speak before, not even in the newsreels. He always seemed to be waving at a crowd from the entrance of a DC-3 about to take off or while reviewing troops as they marched by in the distance.

"Yes, sir. I am." I was worried where this might be leading. *Did it have something to do with Mei-hua's desire to rejoin his enemy, the CCP? How had he learned about that?*

"I have an assignment for you to perform in Shanghai. This probably will be the most important and dangerous investigation you ever will pursue in your lifetime. Are you ready to assist your country and your president?" he asked.

I was relieved. This did not involve Mei-hua. "I am, sir." I relaxed.

Chiang nodded. "What I am about to tell you is top secret. You will not disclose it to anyone. You will die at your country's hand if you ever reveal what I am about to say to you. Do you understand?"

"I do, sir. Yes, I do."

I did not like the sound of this. If Chiang wanted me to do something for him in Shanghai, I couldn't imagine achieving it without disclosing all or some information to other people, as needed. After all, the city was occupied by our enemy, and was existing under severe wartime restrictions. I would probably need help to complete my assignment.

Chiang explained to me that Madam Chiang, while carrying out a top-secret mission for him in Shanghai, had been the target of a failed assassination attempt. He did not tell me the nature of that mission and I did not ask.

"You will investigate the plot and identify the plotters. All the conspirators, no matter where that might lead. I also want to know if Madam Chiang was the target merely as a warning to me or if that attempt actually was the first step in a more elaborate scheme to kill me."

I spoke up for the first time. I had to put this into perspective for him before his expectations became even more unrealistic than they apparently already were.

I felt I had to indicate my concern with what he'd said. I didn't think I would have another chance to do so.

"I doubt what you want is possible, sir," I said. "It's very difficult to move around Shanghai under the Occupation. My PI business is failing because of that situation.

"If I try to investigate this, I probably will be noticed and taken into custody by the Dwarf Bandits. They will assume I am a spy because of all the questions I would have to ask and then pursue in order to investigate this for you."

I paused briefly to give him a chance to respond. He said nothing, but his face and neck darkened.

I continued. "I don't believe it's possible to do what you want, at least not the secret way you want it done."

Chiang's nostrils flared. His face turned dark red. His skin tightened before my eyes.

He spoke to me softly, but with menace in his squeaky voice.

"I am not asking that you do this, Mr. Ling. I am ordering you to do it. You will obey me or, I promise you, you and your loved ones will suffer serious consequences."

"With all due respect, sir, as I explained, I don't possibly see how I can—"

Chiang slammed his fist on his desktop so forcefully I involuntarily jumped. I heard the two soldiers, stationed behind me on either side of the entrance door, engage their rifle bolts.

Chiang's voice, when he spoke, now was an octave higher

and was much more strident than before. He looked into my eyes. He spoke slowly and deliberately, carefully enunciating every word, so each word lingered in the air.

"You will do this for me, Mr. Ling, and you will resolve it very quickly and secretly, or my people in Shanghai will arrest your Communist wife. Then she will be interned and will be shot for being the CCP spy we all know she is.

"And you, Mr. Ling, you will be drafted into the army, with the lowest rank, and will immediately be sent to the front lines to die defending our country. I am not bluffing," he said.

I paused before answering, but not for long. I nodded. "Of course, I'll do it, Mr. President. I'll do this exactly how you said. Secretly and quickly. I will be honored to carry out this mission for you and our country."

Chiang said nothing. He now ignored me and looked down at a paper on his desk.

One of the soldiers walked over and tapped me on my shoulder. He indicated with his head that we were to leave the office. My very-long five minutes with the generalissimo were over.

We reversed this morning's procedure, headed for the airport, and then flew home.

I entered our apartment at about 3:00 a.m. I was exhausted.

I first went to Fen and Ji's bedroom to kiss them in their sleep. Bik slept on the floor in between their beds. She lifted her head, saw I was the intruder, wagged her tail twice, and then returned to sleep.

I went to our room and quietly climbed into bed alongside

Mei-hua. She sighed as I moved close to her. I threw my arm over her shoulder. She never opened her eyes.

I could not fall asleep. My mind would not let go of the threat Chiang had made against Mei-hua and me.

The sun was close to rising. I laid still listening to the sounds of early morning. Birds were beginning to chirp, insects beginning to swarm. I heard the creaking wheels of the heavy cart pushed by the night-soil collector as he passed-by under our window. He was heading to the Whangpoo River to dump his foul-smelling contents onto a waiting barge whose captain will sell the human excrement to farmers, who will use it as manure for their fruits and vegetables.

I closed my eyes and wondered what I'd gotten myself into and why Chiang had selected me. I would have an interesting story to tell Mei-hua when she awoke.

PART TWO

CHAPTER 17

T.V. Soong and Madam Chiang

Current week. Fourth week of June. Chungking.

T.V. Soong and Madam Chiang arranged a hurried meeting in T.V.'s office. He had called the meeting at Generalissimo Chiang's request, although Chiang thought it best that he not attend. Apparently, Chiang and T.V. believed Mei-ling might listen to T.V.'s advice, to save face, even if she would not listen to her husband's advice.

"Your husband is correct, Younger Sister," T.V. said. "You likely are in continuing danger and should keep a low profile for now."

Mei-ling shook her head and gave her brother White Eyes. She slightly lifted her chin, leaned her head back, then rolled her eyes up into her head so only the whites showed. This was the ultimate expression of distain that could be directed by one Celestial at another.

She looked back down and quickly composed herself, staring hard at T.V. "I'll do no such thing." She shook her head.

"In that case, Younger Sister, there is another matter I should like to talk to you about."

Mei-ling frowned.

"The Generalissimo's decision to terminate the Xi'an Agreement and now enter into a treaty with the Kwantung is unpatriotic and risky," T.V. said.

"I don't see how it can ultimately succeed although, on its face, the plan seems possible. In reality, there are many ways his plan can go wrong. Should that occur, it would be a disaster for China.

"You need to support my efforts to talk your husband out of doing this. Let him stick with his agreement with Mao. They can fight one another, as originally agreed at Xi'an, once they've together driven the Dwarf Bandits into the sea."

Madam Chiang shook her head. She placed a cigarette into a thin, ivory cigarette holder, lit the cigarette, and drew heavily on the burning tobacco. She looked back at her brother.

"Take that up with my husband, if you really believe that. It is not my place to second-guess the generalissimo. He is the soldier, not I. The generalissimo knows what is best for our country and how best to achieve it."

CHAPTER 18

Sun-jin

Current week. Fourth week of June. Shanghai.

MEI-HUA AND I ATE BREAKFAST together in the morning after my return from Chungking. Fen and Ji played in another room. Bik curled up under the table with her snout resting on my right foot.

I told Mei-hua everything that had occurred from the time the three men barged into my office until I arrived home in the middle of the night.

"Why didn't you wake me? We could have talked about this."

"I was exhausted. I couldn't have carried on a conversation with you. My attempts would have frustrated us both. I just wanted to close my eyes and sleep."

"Did you sleep?"

"No."

She nodded and took my hand with both hers.

"This sounds like an impossible investigation," she said. "The Dwarf Bandits aren't going to permit you to wander around the city asking questions and snooping as you look into the attack. They might even misunderstand your purpose and decide you're a spy."

"I don't have a choice. I told you what's at stake for us if I don't comply. Chiang has a reputation for living up to his threats. I don't want to find out."

Mei-hua shook her head. "What do you think this really is about? I don't understand why Madam Chiang would even be in enemy territory so she could be attacked there."

"I don't know that yet," I said. "Chiang didn't tell me, but I probably will have to find that out as part of my investigation."

"The assassination attempt might have involved more than just a crime against the Dragon Lady," Mei-hua said. "It also might have involved espionage. Wouldn't that complicate your investigation and place you at great risk?"

I nodded. "Unfortunately, yes, but as I said, what choice do I have?"

"Are you planning on involving Eli in your investigation?"

"If he wants."

"Is that fair given what could happen to you, to us, if you fail?" she said. "Do you really want to drag him into such a dangerous situation?"

"I'll explain everything to him. He can decide if he wants to be part of it."

Eli and I met at Blue Dragon's office. I described the investigation to him, leaving out nothing, including the part about Chiang threatening me and my loved ones if I told anyone.

"That's it," I said. "The good news is we will be well paid for our investigation, whether or not you decide to participate.

The bad news is the inherent risk involved in pursuing this and the dangerous obstacles imposed by the Occupation.

"Those obstacles," I said, "could make it impossible for us to succeed, or, worse, could result in our arrest for spying against the Dwarf Bandits."

Eli shrugged. "Any other bad news?"

"The investigation will likely be both a criminal investigation — which we both are used to — but also possibly will be an espionage investigation — which we have no experience with. In that latter case, the Dwarf Bandits might find reason to arrest us and execute us as spies."

"That certainly would complicate matters," Eli said, as he laughed.

"You need to think hard whether you want to be involved. It's no problem for me if you say no. It probably would be the smart thing to do. You can handle our other work while I'm tied-up with this."

"What other work?" Eli said.

"*Maskee — Right.* So, think about this and give me your answer when you're ready," I said.

"No need to wait. I'm ready. I'll do it."

"What are you smiling at?" I said.

"I think it's ironic that I will be working on an assignment for Chiang and the KMT, given my history as the former editor of the CCP's *Slovo*, and given that I just told Mei-hua I would assist her in the CCP's Resistance movement against the Japanese here in Shanghai."

Mei-hua? I thought. *So much for our understanding she wouldn't raise rejoining the CCP with Eli until we talked about it again.*

"Glad you find some humor in this," I said. "I wish I could."

CHAPTER 19

Big-Eared Tu

One week earlier. Third week of June. Chungking.

Pock-Marked Huang eagerly awaited Big-Eared Tu's description of his plan to block the treaty between Chiang and the Japanese.

"My plan is simple," Tu said. "I expect you to arrange to carry it out."

"Of course, Master Tu," Huang said,

"The generalissimo told me he will be sending T.V. Soong back to Shanghai to oversee the signing of the treaty again.

"You will have Soong assassinated in Shanghai before he leaves to return to Chungking with a signed treaty in his hand. Chiang and his wife will then blame the Dwarf Bandits for his death and will set aside all thoughts of a treaty with those invading vermin."

CHAPTER 20

Eli and Sun-jin

Current week. Fourth week of June. Shanghai.

"So," Eli said, "you've told me about some aspects of the investigation, but really not much at all when you think about what you've said. What's this investigation really about? What aren't you telling me?"

"What I told you is all I know," I said. "I agree, it's not much to go on."

"What was Madam Chiang's secret mission?" Eli said. "If we knew that, knew what she was doing in enemy-controlled Shanghai, perhaps that would help us."

I shook my head. "I have no idea what it was about. Chiang never said, but it must have been very important for him to have sent his wife into enemy territory, endangering her that way. Otherwise, why wouldn't he have sent some expendable diplomat."

Eli nodded. "How did the Kwantung know Madam Chiang would be in Shanghai? Was she there to see them?" Eli said. "Were they behind the attack?"

"You're assuming," I said, "that her mission was with the

Dwarf Bandits, and that they knew she would be here. Maybe the Dwarf Bandits had nothing to do with the attack.

"Perhaps she met with members of the KMT Resistance behind enemy lines, and the attack was unrelated to that meeting, just a Resistance attack on a Kwangtung convoy."

Eli shrugged. "How should we proceed?" he said.

"I see our investigation having two parallel tracks. We have to investigate the Kwantung and any Japanese civilians now present in Shanghai to see if they tried to assassinate Madam Chiang, but we also have to determine if Celestial civilians in Shanghai might have been behind it."

Eli snorted like a dog. He smiled. "Oh, is that all?" he said. "That should be easy to do in an enemy-occupied city."

Eli's sarcasm wasn't helping, but I decided not to say anything. He was, after all, still young.

CHAPTER 21

Sun-jin

Current week. Fourth week of June. Shanghai.

ELI AND I FINISHED OUR meeting at the office. He left, but we agreed to meet again in the afternoon to talk through the case once more. I hoped that in the interval one of us would come up with some ideas how to proceed with the investigation. I felt that so far, I'd achieved next to nothing except to explain the case to him.

Before I left the office to go home and have lunch with Mei-hua and the twins, I called one of my informants, an elderly Celestial who lived in the Old City. He seemed angry that I called him and told me he did not want to hear from me again. He threatened to turn me in for placing him in danger just by asking him to inform for me. I hoped he would not follow through with his threat.

We fed Fen and Ji, fed Bik and filled her water bowl, then sat down together to eat rice and steamed carp. Mei-hua prepared the fish my favorite way: she fried the carp, then allowed it to come to room temperature. Then she bathed it in a sweet and savory mulberry sauce she'd invented, then sprinkled it with toasted sesame seeds. I especially enjoyed the fish head. We each had a glass of *Tiger Wine* — that foul-smelling wine made from tiger bones that have marinated and disintegrated in rice wine — as we ate.

Mei-hua wanted to talk about the case. I wanted to ask her why she had asked Eli to help her with the CCP's Resistance movement although we had agreed she would wait until we had talked again about her rejoining the CCP. But after thinking about it, I decided that talking right now about Chiang's investigation was more important. I would wait until another time for the discussion about Eli.

"How do you plan to proceed?" Mei-hua said.

I shrugged and took a sip of wine. "Trial and error, I suppose. The way all investigations start out until you find some lead to point you in the right direction.

"To get started, I'll call my informants and ask to meet with them. Then, Eli and I will cross into Hongkew to find my former informants. Hopefully, if we can locate them, they will find us some useful information that will suggest how we should proceed. Then we will do the same in Chapei."

Mei-hua smiled. "Just what a spy would do. That's risky."

I nodded. "Unfortunately, yes. But that's the problem with any investigation in enemy-occupied territory. Everything you do to investigate looks like espionage."

Mei-hua reached across the table and squeezed my hand.

"There's something else," I said.

Mei-hua frowned. "Bad news?"

"I've thought about your decision to return to the CCP and join its resistance movement. I don't want you to do this. It would be bad *joss* for our family."

"*Bú! — No!*" Mei-hua said. She released my hand, then closed her hands into tiny fists. "That is not your decision, Sun-jin. It's mine." Her cheeks became red, her voice soft but crisp like sharpened steel.

"I care about our family just as much as you do, so please do not suggest I do not. I understand the risk, but I must take it. I will not be foolish in this undertaking," she said.

I took a deep breath. *Qing, — Please*, listen to me," I said. "This would be too dangerous for you, for all of us. You know, from what I've told you, that the Kwantung will soon be watching me since I will be moving around the city asking questions. That means they will also become aware of you, too.

"It will only be a matter of time before they will find your absences from our home to be curious, and will then watch you, too. Are you willing to put our family at risk like that?"

"Me? I won't be the only one putting our family at risk. So will you. Yet you're willing to do that, Sun-jin? By your own words, you have said you are prepared to do so. So, why not me, too?"

I took another deep breath, held it, then slowly let it out. I felt trapped in this argument. "You know I have no choice. I must pursue Chiang's investigation. To not do so will itself bring great harm to us and our children. You know that."

"And you have no choice in this other matter," Mei-hua said. "It is my decision, not yours. I will make it. I will decide if I return to the CCP and actively join its Resistance against the Dwarf Bandits. Not you."

Mei-hua stood, sharply nodded her head once, then walked around the table to behind my chair. She leaned over, put her hand on my shoulder, and kissed the top of my head. Then she left the room. I heard our bedroom door close behind her.

CHAPTER 22

Generalissimo Chiang Kai-shek

Current week. Fourth week of June. Chungking.

C HIANG KAI-SHEK FOLLOWED HIS SERGEANT-MAJOR to the building's basement. Five guards, all carefully trained over the years to protect Chiang and to reflexively obey his orders, accompanied them.

They arrived at a small, dank room having no windows. Its furnishings consisted of a bare, badly scarred wooden desk with a folding chair behind it. There was another chair placed in the center of the room, positioned directly below a single lightbulb hanging from the ceiling by a thin electrical cord. The chair faced the desk.

Chiang seated himself behind the desk.

"Bring the bandits here," he said.

The sergeant-major saluted, turned, and left the room. He returned within five minutes, accompanied by three blindfolded prisoners, their arms bound behind their backs. Two other guards followed them into the room.

The prisoners' faces and heads were bruised, swollen, and bloody.

"Remove the blindfolds," Chiang said.

The prisoners stood facing Chiang. The guards stood behind them, their rifles at the ready.

Chiang said nothing. He did not look at the prisoners. After a minute passed, he lit a cigarette, stared at it for a few seconds, then looked at the ceiling and blew out a stream of blue smoke. He coughed several times from deep within his chest, then looked at the prisoners.

"You are here," he said, his screechy voice rising in pitch and volume as he spoke, "because you are Communist vermin and were part of a plot to assassinate my wife."

The prisoners stared at the floor in front of them, their heads hung low.

"Look at me when I speak to you, you scum. You will tell me who was behind the attempt to kill my wife, or you will die in this room."

Chiang stood up from his seat, leaned forward on his palms, and looked at each man in his eyes, stopping briefly before moving his gaze to the next prisoner.

He waited. Then he straightened up, drew heavily again on his cigarette, emptied the smoke from his lungs directly at the three men, and said, speaking matter-of-factly, "Sergeant-Major, pick one of these insects and strangle him."

The officer nodded. He grabbed one of the men by his collar, dragged him backwards two meters, then forced him to his knees.

He walked around the man and stood in front of him. He looked over at Chiang.

"I gave you an order, Sergeant-Major," Chiang said. He looked back at the two other prisoners, "Face your foolish comrade. You will watch him die. Then you will follow him if you do not answer my questions."

The sergeant-major removed his field jacket, folded it carefully and laid it on the floor next to the hapless prisoner. He rolled-up his sleeves.

The sergeant-major walked around behind the kneeling prisoner. He placed his hands around the prisoner's throat and neck, his thumbs and fingers pressing against the man's larynx. He slowly squeezed, gradually increasing the pressure.

It took ten seconds for the prisoner to become unconscious, and another three minutes of hard squeezing for the man to die. Two guards removed the body from the room.

The sergeant-major grabbed his field jacket, carefully unfolded it, and slipped it on again. He stood at attention facing Chiang.

The remaining two prisoners turned to face Chiang again as he sat behind the desk. He lit a new cigarette, then sipped from a glass of water.

He looked at the prisoners. "One of you will die next," he said. "The first to disclose the information I want will be permitted to live. The other will not. There will be no second chance."

He looked from one man to the other, slowly moving his eyes from one to the other and back again. He bared yellow-stained teeth.

"I know the plot against my wife was ordered by Mao. What I do not know, but you will tell me, is how he knew about her mission to Shanghai."

Neither prisoner spoke. Sweat covered their faces and soaked their shirts. The acrid smell of urine suddenly pervaded the air.

Chiang waited. He drummed his fingers on the desktop.

After half a minute of silence passed, Chiang said,

"Sergeant-Major, remove one of these men to the other side of this room and blow out his brains. Use my pistol," he said, as he held up his sidearm. "Do it in the corner over there," he said, as he pointed, "to keep his blood and brains off my uniform."

Afterward, Chiang faced the remaining prisoner.

"Still have nothing to say?" he asked.

The man trembled and shook his head. "*Ayeeyah!* I don't know nothing, sir. I would help you if I could. I'm just a lowly officer. I don't know nothing."

Chiang faced the sergeant-major. "Tie the prisoner to that chair," he said, nodding toward the chair under the hanging lightbulb.

"Bind his arms and feet to the chair so he cannot flail. Tape his mouth closed so he cannot scream."

When this had been completed, Chiang said to the sergeant-major, "Give me your garrote." He extended his hand toward the officer.

With this weapon in hand, Chiang moved behind the seated prisoner, looped the wire over his head and around his neck, then twisted the handles until the man was lifeless, his head lolling sideways. Chiang left the weapon dangling from the dead man's partially severed neck.

He turned to the sergeant-major, and said, "Dispose of the bodies in Spotted Serpent Park. The *huang gou — wild dogs* will feast tonight."

CHAPTER 23

Sun-jin

Current week. Fourth week of June. Shanghai.

RETURNED TO THE OFFICE AFTER lunch to meet again with Eli. We had agreed to go our separate ways for a few hours, think about the investigation, then meet again to trade ideas.

Eli wasn't at the office when I arrived. I forced myself to put aside my concern resulting from Mei-hua's decision to return to the CCP and to focus on the case for now.

Since I was a few minutes early, I reviewed my file containing information about our informants and the various coded phrases we used when we contacted each one of them. I had been out of contact with these men for many months. Until this investigation, the few new cases I'd worked under the Occupation had not required the help of informants.

I wanted to consider the best way to contact them under the circumstances of the Occupation. I couldn't just show up at their places of work and insist we talk, as I'd often done before the Occupation.

I went to our wall safe and counted out $500 yuan in small-denomination banknotes to make down payments to those men who were willing to seek information for us. They would receive the balance of their payments if they delivered.

While I waited for Eli to arrive, I called seven of our informants, using their telephone numbers in the file. Three were in Hongkew, the Jewish and Japanese sections of the French Concession; four were in Chapei, the bombed-out Chinese Old City. I hoped I would receive a better response than I received this morning when I called the Celestial who not only turned down my request for help, but also had threatened to inform on me.

I did not make contact with any of the seven men I called.

I looked at my wristwatch. Eli was almost one hour late. That was not like him. Typically, if he was going to be late, he telephoned to alert me. I decided that in wartime, one hour late was not much. It was too soon for me to be concerned about him even in these chaotic and dangerous times.

Almost another hour passed and Eli still hadn't arrived. Now I was worried. I called him at his home to see if he'd forgotten our meeting — not likely since he had never done that before — or if he had mixed up which afternoon we were to meet again — also not likely since we made the appointment only a few hours ago this very morning. There was no answer at his home.

I waited another fifteen minutes, was about to call his home again, when the office door opened.

I looked up expecting Eli to walk in, full of apologies or, at least, with an explanation.

It was not Eli who stepped into our office.

It was his father, Avram Ben-David Reuben.

My back stiffened. I could feel the color drain from my face.

"Welcome, my friend," I said, frowning. "Sit." I gestured toward the old sofa we keep in our client waiting area.

Avram did not look happy. His face was red, his eyes narrowed. I was concerned since he was here in Eli's place. That meant something had happened to Eli that prevented him from being here.

He did not move toward the sofa.

"*Ayeeyah!* Is Eli all right?" I said.

"We need to talk. It concerns Eli."

"Please, let's sit," I said again. He sat. I pulled up a chair to face him.

"The Kwantung arrested Eli just after you left your meeting with him this morning. Apparently, they came here looking for you, but you had already left. They took Eli instead."

Why would the Dwarf Bandits come here looking for me? I wondered. *I hadn't even set about my investigation yet, hadn't started asking questions that might seem suspicious. It made no sense unless the Celestial I called had informed on me as he threatened to do.*

"Where is he now?" I said. "Can we have him released? Can your rabbi help? I understand he's on good terms with the Kwantung."

"He's already been released. Our rabbi called in some favors with the Kwantung, and Eli was set free. He's home now, pretty shaken up, but otherwise all right."

"Why did the Kwantung want to see me?" I asked. "And why did they take Eli if they really wanted me?"

"I don't know why they wanted to see you. They wanted

Eli to tell them where they could find you. He refused, so they arrested him.

Why didn't they just come to my home when they didn't find me at my office? I'm listed in the city directory and am registered with the collaboration-police as required.

It occurred to me that maybe they were at my home waiting for me now, frightening Mei-hua and the children by their presence there. I had to call home as soon as Avram left.

Avram sighed and continued. "Eli was fortunate this time. He might not be so lucky again," Avram said. "The fact is, my friend, I don't want my son working with you anymore. It's just too dangerous in these times."

Because Avram had been the one who first suggested that Eli come work with me, and even though he and I have been friends for many years, I was tempted to tell him to mind his business and let his adult son make that decision. But I didn't say that. I would have said the same thing to him as he did if I were in his place, if it was my son we were talking about.

"Does Eli agree with you?" I said.

"No."

"Is he going to follow your wish?"

"I doubt it, so I want you to discourage him. Tell him you cannot afford to pay his salary any longer, that he has to find some other work."

"We've already been through that discussion this morning because it's true," I said. I summarized my previous conversation with Eli on this subject.

Avram stood. "I don't know what else I can do then. Please be careful and watch out for my boy."

He extended his hand and we shook, our friendship still

intact, but perhaps a little more tenuous than it had been before his visit.

As soon as Avram left I called home and spoke to our *amah*. She said that Mei-hua was at the food market to try to buy dinner for tonight, and that the children were playing in their room.

"Did we have any visitors this afternoon?" I said.

"No, Master Sun-jin, none."

That relieved my mind a bit.

CHAPTER 24

Sun-jin

Current week. Fourth week of June. Shanghai.

A VRAM HAD LEFT MY OFFICE. I thought about what he'd said.

He was right, of course. Eli would be in danger as long as he worked with me on this assignment. I was in constant, potential danger myself because of it, but I had no choice but to investigate. Eli had a choice. He had nothing to lose by walking away. I would walk away if I were him.

I decided I would take him off the case if he ever returned to our office.

I called two more of my informants, using telephone numbers that had always worked for us before the Occupation. One number was assigned to a café in Chapei where the informant had worked as a waiter. I gave the agreed-upon coded phrase to the person who answered, and waited for my informant to come to the phone.

After a few minutes, someone picked up the receiver and said, speaking Hu, "Chun Lin no longer work here. He is gone long time, many months." The speaker replaced the receiver in its cradle, breaking our connection before I could ask questions to pursue his statement.

My call to my informant in Hongkew was even less successful. As soon as I delivered the coded phrase, the person on the other end hung up on me, breaking the connection.

That left me twelve more informants to try. I called them all, but didn't reach any of them. At least I wasn't abruptly cut off. I would try again later.

I decided to return home to spend time with Mei-hua, Fen, Ji, and Bik. Who knew, once my investigation really got going, how long it would be before I would have that luxury again.

I stepped into the hallway outside my office. I had just closed and locked the door behind me when I heard the lift's bell ring once and its doors open. I turned and looked to see who was entering the hallway. I hoped it would be Eli.

Two Kwantung soldiers stepped from the lift, followed by an officer, and then by two more infantry soldiers.

The officer looked at me, and said, "*Hai!* That's him. Take him."

CHAPTER 25

Eli

Current week. Fourth week of June. Shanghai.

"I UNDERSTAND WHAT YOU TOLD ME, Eli," his father said. "I, too, was young and foolish once. That doesn't mean, however, I have to agree with your decision. I don't. Rejoining the CCP is dangerous and reckless."

Avram sat down, but immediately stood again. He pinched the skin of his throat several times.

It was clear to Eli that his father was worried about him, not angry.

Eli let out the breath he'd been holding. He knew his father would not put up much of a fight to keep him from rejoining the CCP, but he did not want to unnecessarily worry him.

"I won't do anything reckless, *Abba*, Eli said, using the Hebrew term for father. "You have my word. Probably all I'll be engaged in is writing and publishing a periodic newsletter. I'll keep my head down, maintain a low profile."

Eli could see his father's resolve melting away as they talked. Avram sighed, sat again, and shook his head once. He looked up at Eli, who stood across the room.

"Who will tell *Ima*?" Avram said, using the Hebrew word

for mother. "She has to know although she will constantly worry about you. We cannot keep this a secret from her. I am willing to do so if you wish."

Eli knew his father well. He saw this as his father's test of his resolve. If he was afraid to be the one who revealed his plans to his mother, his father would see his decision as a young man's romantic escapade, not as the serious undertaking it was for him. In that event, Eli knew, his father would again begin his efforts to talk him out of his decision.

"I will tell *Ima*," Eli said.

His father nodded approvingly.

Their dispute was over.

CHAPTER 26

Generalissimo Chiang Kai-shek

Current week. Fourth week of June. Chungking.

As worried and angry as he was by the assassination attempt against his wife, Chiang was not deterred from his mission with the Dwarf Bandits. He assumed that the attack either was an attack against him — that the plotters had expected him to be in the car with Mei-ling — or that it was a message to him delivered via the attack against his wife.

In either case, he was not concerned by its implicit meaning. He had been the subject of plots before, directly and indirectly, his entire military and political careers. He knew he would be a target again, but he still believed in his original plan, and he intended to resurrect his stalled treaty with the Kwantung.

He called a meeting with his wife and T.V.

They met in a secret, soundproofed room located one floor above Chiang's office. An armed guard stood outside the closed door.

"*Shi — Yes, T.V.,*" Chiang said, looking first at his brother-in-law, then at Madam Chiang, then back again at T.V., "you heard me right. I still intend to enter into a treaty with the Dwarf Bandits. The sooner the better, particularly if Mao or the CCP-vermin were behind the attempt to kill Mei-ling."

"Are the Kwantung's leaders still interested?" T.V. said.

"It doesn't matter if they are or are not," Chiang said. "You will convince them they should be interested, that it still is in their best interest to join me in this."

T.V. looked at his sister, paused, then said, "Should Mei-ling join me on this trip? After all, she was successful before in convincing the Kwantung to sign the treaty."

"No. It would be too dangerous for her. You will undertake the trip by yourself, but with two KMT undercover agents to protect you."

T.V. nodded. "May I suggest, Generalissimo, "that this trip might be more likely to succeed if you will stop spreading rumors that Kwangtung generals tried to assassinate your wife. Instead, spend a week or two planting a different story — that you are close to arresting the would-be murderers, who were among your officers.

"Say they were plotting against you, and thought you were in the car with my sister. Then arrest and publicly execute two or three of your staff generals. Do that with great fanfare and allow that story to circulate for a few weeks in Shanghai. That should help the Kwantung save face and bring them around again."

"I don't have a few weeks," Chiang said. "I want this achieved in the next few days. Start the process so you can go to Shanghai. I will expect to have a signed document in my hands by week's end."

T.V. raised an eyebrow as he glanced over at his sister, who had been uncommonly quiet during this exchange.

She shrugged her shoulders slightly. Mei-ling knew better than to challenge her husband's decisions, other than in the privacy of their bed.

T.V. would go to Shanghai to revive the treaty.

CHAPTER 27

Sun-jin

Current week. Fourth week of June. Shanghai.

I TURNED TO FACE THE SOLDIERS as they raced up the hall toward me. My back tightened and I began to sweat. Remembering my days as a policeman dealing with people I was about to arrest, I made sure my hands were in plain sight, my palms clearly open.

As the soldiers came close, I slowly raised my arms above my head. I made no sudden movements.

The soldiers promptly surrounded me. The officer — a Kwantung colonel — slowly walked up the hallway toward me. He looked me up and down as he approached. He stopped when he was two meters away.

"You are Ling Sun-jin?" he said.

I nodded. "I am. May I show you my papers?"

He nodded.

I lowered my right arm and reached into my pocket. I pulled out my ID-card.

He took it from me, looked at the card and then at me, then handed the ID back.

"*Hai!* We will go into your office and talk," he said, speaking heavily accented Hu. He pointed toward the locked office door. "Unlock the door so we do not have to break it open."

The officer, the soldiers, and I walked into my office.

The colonel seated himself behind my desk. I stood on the other side facing him. The soldiers arranged themselves around the room, looking toward us.

"You will tell me the truth when I ask you questions. Do you understand?"

I nodded again.

"Are you a member of the enemy KMT?" he said.

"No."

"Are you a spy?"

"Of course not." My back became rigid.

The colonel ignored my answer, and said softly, as if he wanted to be my confidant, "Who are you spying for? You can tell me. The KMT? The CCP? The Round-Eyes, perhaps?"

He now looked hard in my eyes as his left hand moved to the hilt of the saber hanging from his belt.

"*Ayeeyah!* I'm not a spy," I said, trying to keep my mounting fear out of my voice. "I'm just a Chinese citizen, a private investigator, working from this office, struggling under the Occupation to make a living for my family."

The colonel's voice now seemed strained with impatience when he said, "Why have you been contacting your former informants, looking for one named Chun Lin, probably others, too?"

I could feel my eyes open wide. *So Chun Lin did inform on me, after all.* "I am starting a new investigation. I hoped he might help me find information. He has been one of my sources in the past."

The colonel said nothing. He stared at me as if waiting for

more explanation. After a few seconds, he said, "Chun Lin no longer wants to work for you. He reported you to me. Why did you call him?"

"As I said, sir, I called him for help on a new case. No other reason. I wanted his help."

"Tell me about the case."

I had no choice but to lie. "Someone stole a valuable, collectible postage stamp from a stamp vendor in Hongkew. I've been hired to locate it and to return the stamp to its owner."

"And have you located it?"

"Not yet."

This line of questioning and my similar answers continued for several minutes. Finally, the colonel faced the guards and spoke to one of them in Japanese. I did not understand what he said.

The soldier came over to me, followed by another.

One of the men grunted something I did not understand, but also made a gesture with his arm that I did understand. He wanted me to follow him out of my office.

The two soldiers led me from my office into our small waiting room. I could hear the dialing of my desk telephone, followed by the officer speaking Japanese.

After a few minutes the colonel called out to the guards watching me, and the soldiers led me back into my office. One soldier shoved me twice from behind as we returned to my office.

I again stood before the seated colonel.

"If I find you lied to me," he said, again speaking Hu, "I will arrest you and intern you in a camp until you are executed for spying. Do you understand me?"

"I'm not lying. I am not a spy," I said.

We will see, the colonel thought. *I will give you the chance to hang yourself and your fellow conspirators by leading me to them. I will have you watched.*

"From now on," the colonel said, "you will not roam the city outside the former Settlement, not even to investigate your cases. I order you to stay within these boundaries. If you disobey me, you will arrested as a spy. Do you understand."

I nodded. "I do."

I wondered why this officer, who had the power to arrest me, didn't just do so right now instead of warning me. He could then ship me off to an internment camp and be done with me. We Celestials have been interned for far flimsier reasons than this.

The colonel and soldiers left my office.

CHAPTER 28

Sun-jin

Current week. Fourth week of June. Shanghai.

A FTER THE SOLDIERS LEFT MY office, I also left. I boarded the electric streetcar to go home, have lunch, and spend time with Mei-hua and our children. I had a headache and was in no mood to work right then. By the time I reached home, I was in a foul mood.

Mei-hua had already fed Fen, Ji, and Bik, so she and I were able to share a meal alone. This gave me the opportunity to fill her in on my day so far.

"You look ill," she said. "Come, let me feed you."

"There's much to tell you," I said.

Mei-hua poured us the last of the *Tiger Wine* we had opened the other day.

I described Avram's surprise visit to me, and our conversation concerning Eli, including Eli's visit from the Dwarf Bandits who were looking for me.

"What do you plan to do if Eli now shows up?"

"I'll tell him about the conversation I had with his father, and will tell him that as far as I'm concerned, the decision is up to him. I'm fine with whatever he decides, although, I'll also tell him I hope he will decide to stay and continue to work with me."

I told Mei-hua about the visit from the Kwantung colonel and his soldiers.

"There is no way you can avoid being hurt," she said, "either by Chiang or by the Dwarf Bandits. It seems you're trapped between them."

I nodded. "I am."

"What can you do about it?" she said.

"I'll investigate as planned, without regard to the Kwantung. I'll do my best to keep a low profile and will look into the case as Chiang insisted. If I don't, he surely will harm us. The Kwantung, on the other hand, might or might not harm us, even if they do find out I've left the Settlement as part of my investigation.

"One thing is for sure. I cannot shut down the investigation. For me to do so would not escape Chiang's ears. He has spies everywhere."

Mei-hua retrieved Fen and Ji from their bedroom, and brought them into the kitchen with us. Bik followed on her own, wagging her tail when she saw me. I leaned over and rubbed her back.

As usual, Fen ran right up to me, climbed up onto my lap, and said, "I want to play with you." Then she kissed me on the cheek. Ji, as usual, stayed back, away from me and Fen, his head slightly bowed. He looked at me from heavily-lidded eyes. I smiled and extended my hand toward him.

"Come here, Little Ji. Give me a kiss." I patted my lap and

moved Fen over to one side so there would be room for them both.

Bik, sensing the mood, stood on her back legs and put her front paws on my knee. She wagged her tail furiously and licked my hand.

CHAPTER 29

Sun-jin

Current week. Fourth week of June. Shanghai.

AFTER LUNCH, AFTER FEN AND Ji had gone back into their shared bedroom to take their afternoon naps, I placed calls to the informants I hadn't yet spoken with.

Of these twelve calls, only two were successful. Either the remaining ten people had moved or, perhaps, were casualties of the war. I'd likely never know.

I realized I will have to recruit and groom new informants if I am going to continue in the PI business. *This probably won't be possible under current conditions,* I thought. *Hopefully, Mao and Chiang will soon defeat the Dwarf Bandits and end the Occupation.*

One of the informants I reached lived in the bombed-out Old City. This informant was an elderly Celestial who, as a young man, had failed his state exams in his effort to become a government bureaucrat. As a result of this failure — and because his failure had caused his family and village to lose face — his family and village had long since disowned him. He could not return home.

Like many other such young men in this predicament — at

least those many who had not taken their own lives — my informant was forced to earn his living as a professional letter writer, sitting behind a flimsy folding table along Nanking Road, taking on Shanghai's illiterate Celestials as temporary clients, writing letters home for them.

The other informant — a Dwarf Bandit — lived and worked in Hongkew. This was the section of Shanghai inhabited mainly by Dwarf Bandits, but also by Jewish refugees who had fled the Nazis before the world war. These wretched immigrants had recently been herded by the Dwarf Bandits into a small, crowded Ghetto in Hongkew where they worked and lived. This was the Dwarf Bandits' alternative to shipping them to Germany, as demanded by the Nazis.

I went to see my Dwarf-Bandit informant first. I needed to talk to him before he changed his mind about cooperating with me. He had been reluctant to see me when I called, reminding me that he'd told me the last time we talked (many months ago) that he was finished helping me, that he had fully repaid his moral indebtedness to me for once having helped his son out of a jam with the Green Gang.

I couldn't blame him. For one thing, when he informed for me before, we were not at war with the Dwarf Bandits. At least not as openly and as fully as we are now. Had his role helping me back then been discovered, he would have been a pariah among his community, but that would have been all. There would not have been any criminal or more severe penalties for him to face.

Now, of course, China and Japan are involved in full-blown hostilities. If he is caught aiding me now, he likely would be treated as a traitor, and would be dealt with as if he were a spy. The result would be death by firing squad or hanging.

He certainly had a point, but I was desperate for his help. My resources were limited under the Occupation.

He and I met at the Single-Blossom Tea House on Rue du Consulat in Frenchtown where, presumably, neither of us was known, so we would not be recognized. It was dangerous enough, as a general matter under the Occupation, for a Celestial and a Dwarf Bandit to be seen together unless the Celestial's hands were bound behind his back and the Dwarf Bandit was pointing a gun at him. To meet casually, as we planned to do, invited curiosity and danger.

He noisily stomped his foot when we sat down at a table in the corner of the main room.

"*Hai!* You must not contact me again. I told you I am through with you. I have repaid my debt many times now. I am in great danger just meeting with an enemy Celestial. We are done after this."

"Then let's not waste time," I said. "Perform this last assignment for me. I'll pay you well. Then you'll never hear from me again."

He opened and closed his fist even as he looked me in my eyes. "What is it you want?" He looked around the room to see if anyone was watching us.

"There was an attack on Woosung Road last week, not far from the airport. A five-car convoy came under fire. One car burned, killing its occupants."

He raised his eyebrows. "So what. We're in a state of war. Attacks occur every day. What do you expect in these times?"

"This was different. It was a secret convoy being run by the Kwantung, with two civilian cars as part of it," I said.

He shrugged, but said nothing, seemingly indifferent to the distinction. He clearly wasn't interested in helping me.

"I want to know who was responsible for the attack and why."

I handed him some yuan as a down-payment for his information. I promised him gold coins for the balance of his payment if he came through.

He looked around. Satisfied no one was watching us, he stood and left, not saying goodbye to me.

Later that same day I met with my Celestial informant who lived and worked in the Old City. It had been quite a while since I'd been to Chapei.

I rode a rickshaw to the border of Chapei. Then, having been informed by my coolie-puller that he would not enter the Old City because it was too dangerous, too much crime, I left the rickshaw and walked through the filth and stench of the bombed-out streets, dodging water dripping from washing hanging overhead as I did so.

I had the feeling several times I was being watched, specifically watched or followed, not merely observed in general as I walked to my destination. Although I tried to pay attention, and several times quickly turned around to look behind me, I never saw anyone paying attention to me. Just the usual inhabitants of the streets, likely nearby residents, and an occasional, uniformed Dwarf-Bandit soldier wandering the streets, I supposed, as part of his occupation duty.

I met my informant at the Willow Pattern Tea House.

The tea house, built during the Ming Dynasty, but restored in 1855, sits on pilings in the middle of the Whangpoo River. It is notorious for its long wooden bridge, called the Bridge of Nine Turnings, one must walk across to get from the riverbank to the tea house.

The wooden bridge makes nine, abrupt, left and right-angle turns as it stretches over the river. It is configured this way to frustrate and deter evil spirits so they will not attempt to enter the tea house because, as everyone knows, evil spirits prefer to travel in a straight line.

My informant and I settled on cushions set on the floor opposite each other in a private room far from the building's entrance. We were more relaxed together than my Dwarf-Bandit informant and I had been this morning. This is because there is nothing suspicious about two Celestial men having tea together on a cloudy afternoon.

"It is a pleasure to see you again, Sun-jin. You look well considering these trying times."

I bowed my head slightly to acknowledge his ritualistic, Taoist compliment.

"And you, too, Uncle," I said, using the honorific title we Celestials address older men by if we are not related to them. That done, I had met my Confucian obligation to return his greeting and to give him good face.

We then got down to business.

I explained the attack on the convoy without disclosing who, of importance, had been in one of the cars. I said that a special mission had been undertaken at the time (without disclosing the nature of the mission, of course, since I had no idea what that nature might be) and without disclosing who had directed the undertaking of that mission.

I said I was looking for the names of everyone involved — Shanghainese, Dwarf Bandits, Round-Eyes or otherwise — in any and all aspects of the ambush. Everyone. I promised him a large reward for useful information, stating that the size of his reward would depend on his speed of delivery of the information to me, and on the quality of his information. Both were important. I handed over his yuan down-payment.

He promised to turn right to his assignment.

I left the tea house and headed back to my office. I sat down on a bench not far from the tea house and waited for an electric streetcar to come along. *No more bone-jarring rides in a rickshaw for me today*, I thought.

I heard the sound of the streetcar approaching before it rounded the corner and I could see it. I stood up from the bench I had been sitting on and watched as the trolley slowed down. Its metal wheels screeched on the metal tracks. Sparks flew from the connection it made with the overhead electric wires.

As I was about to climb aboard, I noticed a Celestial man across the street. He was watching me.

The man was dressed in an ill-fitting, black, double-breasted suit. He wore a black Fedora on his head. He stared intensely at me, but when my eyes met his, he quickly looked away and feigned disinterest.

Was he a plain-clothes member of the Kwantung assigned to watch me by the colonel who had come to my office and questioned me? Was he to report back whether or not, as part of my investigation, I disobeyed the colonel's orders and had wandered outside the International Settlement?

I was worried about this, but realized I had no choice other than to continue with my assignment. I would have to be more careful as I moved about the city to avoid tipping my hand to this man I believed was following me.

I glanced at him one more time, then boarded the streetcar.

CHAPTER 30

Big-Eared Tu

Current week. Fourth week of June. Chungking.

Tu paced the Great Room, drawing heavily on his opium pipe as he walked. His caged lucky crickets and caged songbirds were silent, sensing the tension in the air.

Tu had been forced into a corner by his subordinate Huang, and he did not like being there. Indeed, he resented being there.

He and Pock-Marked Huang had never actually been friends. They had only been business associates, who accepted and tolerated each other.

When Huang headed the Green Gang in the late 1920s, he recruited Tu into the criminal triad and rapidly promoted him as Tu succeeded at one assignment after another. It did not take long — only seven years — for Tu to rise to the top of the triad and to displace Huang as the Green Gang's leader.

Then, in an act that might have seemed charitable to outsiders, Tu arranged to have Huang become chief of police in the French Concession, an act that gave Tu unlimited authority within the former French treaty-port enclave.

"You have let me down," Tu said to Pock-Marked Huang. "You failed me."

Huang stared at the floor, his hands clasped in front of him. "I apologize, Master Tu. I am prepared to accept the consequences."

Tu sat down on a silk cushion and stared at Huang. Huang continued to stand, his eyes focused on his sandals.

Tu drew heavily on his opium pipe. *For all his failings, Huang has been loyal to me*, he thought. *He still can be useful to me if I use him correctly.*

Tu spoke softly, his voice laced with menace. "I do not tolerate failure," he said. "I expected Soong to be dead while still in Shanghai, not back here with Chiang and Chiang's wife, carrying the signed treaty in his hand."

Huang squirmed, knowing the types of penalties Tu imposed for failure.

"Yes, Master Tu. I fully intended to ambush and kill Soong before he could return to Chungking, but our intelligence in Shanghai was faulty," Huang said. "T.V. was not in the convoy we expected him to be in. The convoy we attacked was a deliberate decoy. I have since dealt with the informant who passed on the misleading information."

Tu nodded, and stared across the room at his caged songbirds. He turned back to Huang.

"And, what," he said, as he stared hard into Huang's eyes, "should I do with you?"

CHAPTER 31

Sun-jin

Current week. Fourth week of June. Shanghai.

DRESSED IN A WORN, SOMEWHAT faded suit jacket with a hole in one elbow (its suit pants had worn out at the beginning of the war, and I had thrown them away when holes appeared in their seat) and an old necktie — my only necktie. I groomed my hair with Brylcreem pomade. I buffed my shoes with a rag made from a worn-out shirt I no longer wore. Then I headed to the office to look at a file before going out to do some snooping.

I reviewed my notes in the case file, then decided it was time to investigate.

As I approached the door to leave, it opened. Eli walked in.

"Forget whatever my father said to you," he said. "I intend to continue here as a PI and to work on Chiang's case with you."

"Good," I said. "Let's get out of here and do some work. I'll catch you up as we walk."

CHAPTER 32

T.V. Soong

Current week. Fourth week of June. Chungking.

T.V. AND MADAM CHIANG WERE back with Chiang in his secret office.

"I was successful," T.V. said. "The Dwarf Bandits re-signed the treaty. I have two counterparts of the document for you to sign. I will return one to Shanghai."

Chiang nodded.

"Within twenty-four hours after I have delivered a fully signed copy of the treaty to the Dwarf Bandits, the cease fire will quietly go into effect throughout China. No one will know this except us," he said, nodding at Chiang and Madam Chiang, "and selected Kwantung diplomats, of course. Not even your generals, who we no longer can trust with this secret, will know."

Chiang reached into his pocket and pulled out his fountain pen. He extended his hand toward T.V. and grabbed for the two documents. Soong handed him the partially signed copies of the treaty.

"The Dwarf Bandits said they will reallocate many of their

troops away from coastal cities and will pursue Mao and his Eighth Route Army in the mountains," T.V. said.

"Excellent," Chiang said. He stroked his close-cropped moustache. He looked at Mei-ling, nodded once at her, smiled briefly, then turned again to face T.V.

"The only problem I encountered, Generalissimo, was that our convoy was attacked on its way back to the airport in Shanghai. Fortunately, based on Mei-ling's experience, we had sent a decoy convoy ahead. We need to know who is trying to block this treaty."

Chiang ignored T.V.'s statement, saying to him, "You are to leave immediately for Shanghai to deliver the signed treaty back to the Kwantung diplomat in charge.

"In the meantime, I will prepare our strategy to attack Mao and the CCP from the mountains opposite where the Dwarf Bandits will hit them. Soon, I expect, Mao and the CCP will be no more."

He grinned. "Soon we will crush the CCP vermin between our forces and the Dwarf Bandits' army. Then we will drive the Dwarf Bandits out of China."

CHAPTER 33

Sun-jin

Current week. Fourth week of June. Shanghai.

MY CELESTIAL INFORMANT WAS THE first to contact me and set up a meeting. He reminded me that I would have to pay him the balance due for his time. I frowned at that statement. This did not bode well. I would have preferred it if he'd said I would have to pay him for his information, not for his time.

We met at L'Art d'Orient, on Bubbling Well Road in the Settlement. This was a well-respected curio and antiques store known the world over as a tourists' trap. It catered to naïve Round-Eyes who wanted to take a piece of the Orient home with them. Its motto was expressed on a large sign that hung over its entrance. The sign famously said, We buy junk; we sell antiques. Tourists — before the war, when there still were tourists — seemed to especially enjoy that sign. It did not seem to deter them. They flocked to the shop as if to seek a mislabeled treasure hiding among the junk.

We met in the private backroom, a place open to visitors only if they had the owner's permission. My informant and the owner seemed to be well-acquainted.

"My money, please, Sun-jin," my informant said, as he extended his palm to me.

I dropped three gold coins into his palm. He had said to me when we first met for this assignment that he no longer accepted paper yuan because of inflation. I would have to pay him using gold.

He raised the coins to his mouth, one at a time, and bit them. Satisfied the coins were not made from gold-plated lead, he dropped the coins into a small leather bag he wore around his neck, pulled the drawstring tight, and slipped the bag down his chest, beneath the folds of the dark green Mandarin-type gown he wore.

"*Ayeeyah!*" I said, impatient to know his information, "Get on with it. What have you learned?"

"Nothing."

"Nothing? Nothing at all?"

"Nothing that will be useful to you. The ambush was an event of war, nothing more than a coincidence involving the Dragon Lady, who was in Shanghai for some unknown reason. It was a non-event of war."

I believed he believed this.

I did not.

I next met with my reluctant Dwarf-Bandit informant.

We met in Frenchtown in the Hongkew Market, the sprawling three-floor shopping emporium owned by Pock-Marked Huang. The market was located within a short walk of the Garden Bridge and the Whangpoo River, within sight of the once-famous Broadway Mansions luxury apartment house.

The market — open twenty-four hours each day, seven days

a week — had been famous before the war for its vast and varied inventory of goods and services. It had offered everything from food prepared in the manner of differing provinces, household goods, lucky charms and lucky crickets, clothing, rare herbs and medicines, livestock, opium and heroin, flower-seller girls, and ice cream.

Unfortunately, since 1937 when the war began, stocks of everything except for flower-seller girls and opium have been in short supply, and, if available at all, were very expensive.

I expected that the emporium would be as safe as any place to meet in Shanghai since Dwarf Bandits and Celestials continued to crowd its floors, even as the ability to successfully shop there for most of us had lessened. It was the perfect cover.

We stood side-by-side at a fish seller's stall, not looking at each other as we talked.

"You now have your money," I said. "Talk to me."

"The attack you described was not a special attack," he said, barely moving his lips, not looking at me as he spoke.

He looked down at a mackerel as he talked. He bent over and touched his fingertips to the fish's iced skin.

"It was an ambush by a Resistance terrorist group who happened to see the small military convoy as it moved through the city, and raced to head it off and attack it. The assault was a normal event of war. That's all. The organizers remain unknown."

I left the Dwarf Bandit and returned to my office. I was getting nowhere fast.

CHAPTER 34

Eli

Current week. Fourth week of June. Shanghai.

ELI WAS BACK AT HIS job as a PI, full of enthusiasm, as always, making his own way through Chiang's investigation, learning from his occasional minor mistakes, by watching me as I operated, and by talking with me about the case.

He began his independent action by involving his brethren in the Jewish Ghetto.

These stateless refugees and the Japanese had maintained close, warm relations ever since the early twentieth century when the Wall Street Jewish financier, Jacob Schiff, helped underwrite the Russo-Japanese War on behalf of the Japanese Emperor.

As a result, the Japanese were — and have remained ever since — convinced that these Jewish bankers had saved Japan's small empire in the East from destruction by the Russians, this at a time when everyone else in the West had turned down the Emperor's requests for war loans.

Eli approached his father about the investigation, seeking his aid with the Jewish community.

"I will need your help, Father, even though I know you prefer I not be involved in PI work."

"Speak to me, Eli. I am resigned to your decision. Of course I will help you if I can. You know I am here for you."

Eli first swore his father to secrecy, then explained the nature of the investigation to him.

"Will you use your contacts in our community to see what you can learn for me?"

"Of course, my son, but based on what you've told me, I do not expect great results."

CHAPTER 35

Sun-jin

Current week. Fourth week of June. Shanghai.

E LI AND I WERE BACK at our office. We had decided to put our heads together to see if we could formulate a list of people likely to try to murder Madam Chiang. We then would eliminate whoever we could from that list. We then would focus on the people left over.

"I vote for Mao and the CCP," Eli said. "What better way to strike at Chiang, indirectly, of course, so as not to openly undermine the Xi'an Agreement? The death of Chiang's wife would shake the generalissimo to his core."

I shook my head. "I don't think so. I have two problems with your hypothesis," I said.

I briefly considered my words. I did not want to offend Eli by showing his hypothesis to be obviously wrong. I also did not want to discourage him from exploring new ideas, no matter how strange or unlikely they might be, since that often was the path to success in investigations.

"If Mao and the CCP wanted to assassinate Madam Chiang as a way to get at the generalissimo, it would have been easier to achieve that in Chungking," I said, "rather than in enemy-occupied Shanghai."

"And the other problem?"

"The generalissimo said Madam Chiang's mission was a secret. How would Mao or the CCP even know she was in Shanghai?"

"Perhaps they learned of it from their informants, and decided to divert blame from themselves by killing her away from Chungking," Eli said. "Then the blame would fall on the Kwantung."

"Perhaps," I said, "We should consider that possibility, but I'm not convinced."

"Could this have been a home-grown plot, Shanghai-based, created here by some of Chiang's many enemies?" Eli said. "Or, maybe by his generals to overthrow him and replace him with one of them?"

"That's more likely," I said. "It's also possible Chiang's generals — or some of them — having learned of the mission — whatever it was — saw this as a way to protest it and, at the same time, as a way to blame the Dwarf Bandits for Madam Chiang's death." I thought about this as I said it. "This is high on my list of possibilities," I said.

"I have another thought," Eli said. "If what you just said is true, isn't it just as probable that the generals were not Chiang's generals, but were Kwantung generals acting for the same reason as Chiang's officers might have, but from the Japanese point of view?"

"That's possible, too."

"In that case," Eli said, "it would be easier for them to cause Madam Chiang's death in Occupied Shanghai than it would be in enemy-occupied Chungking. We need to consider this possibility more closely."

PART THREE

CHAPTER 36

Sun-jin

Current week. Fourth week of June. Shanghai.

ELI AND I FINISHED OUR meeting. I invited him to come with me to visit my brother, Sun-yu. We left our office and rode the electric streetcar to Frenchtown where Elder Brother's nightclub — *The Heavenly Palace* — is located.

As we approached the club, Eli said, "Do you remember bringing me here when you first started teaching me to be a PI?"

"I remember you couldn't take your eyes off the Sing-Song girls sitting at the bar."

Eli blushed.

I patted Eli on his shoulder and laughed.

"That visit was the first step in your education as a PI," I said. "Learning to blend in at the places where you're likely to find and cultivate informants, but don't otherwise want to be noticed."

We entered the club and walked to Elder Brother's office in the back.

Elder Brother looked up when I knocked on his open door. "*Wu an, Younger Brother — Good afternoon, Younger*

Brother," Sun-yu said, as we entered his office. "What brings you to my world of entertainment? I assume this is not a social call."

He looked at Eli, and nodded, then looked back at me.

"*Ayeeyah!* Sun-yu," I said, "Cannot a brother just visit his brother without having some underlying motive up his sleeve? You've become too cynical."

"Never mind," Sun-yu said. He smiled. "As always, I'm happy to see you." He looked at Eli. "And also your young friend here. We haven't met."

"This is Eli, my PI partner," I said, as I turned my head toward Eli. "Eli, this is my brother, Sun-yu. We family members call him, Elder Brother."

They shook hands.

Sun-yu said, "I'll fetch us some *Tiger Wine*. Then we'll see what you want from me."

We drank the wine and toasted our parents and each other. Apparently, Eli had never tasted *Tiger Wine* before. He took one swallow, coughed, and made a pained faced. He set his glass down on the table. He did not put the glass to his lips again during our visit.

Elder Brother, although he no longer smoked, maintained a stock of the most expensive and elusive brands of cigarettes to selectively dole out to his best customers. He offered us each a *Great Wall* cigarette made by the British-American Tobacco company, a Western firm that used to do business in Shanghai before the Occupation. Its officers operating in Shanghai were said to have been interned by the Dwarf Bandits.

The cigarettes had a pleasurable, distinct taste, but now could only be found — and rarely at that — at great expense on the black market. Yet Elder Brother always seemed to have a ready supply of them on hand. I assume he obtained them through his underworld contacts.

Eli and I each eagerly took one and lit up. Then I got down to business.

"We need your help, Elder Brother. We are in the middle of an investigation, but the limitations caused by its sensitivity and by the restrictions inherent in the Occupation have blocked our ability to proceed. We aren't able to investigate the case as we would in normal times."

"I'm not surprised. But isn't that true of all your investigations under the Occupation?"

"More or less, but because this one is especially sensitive, the usual Occupation restrictions seem more onerous. Besides, this is only my fifth case since the Dwarf Bandits occupied Shanghai. Business has been terrible."

"How can I help you?" Elder Brother said.

"I'm hoping you will call upon your underworld contacts to obtain information for me or to point me toward people who will be able and willing to help me."

"Ah," Sun-yu said, "the usual, I see. Tell me about the investigation."

I poured us each another glass of wine and offered Eli a beer, but he declined. I lit a new cigarette for myself. I handed one to Eli.

I told Elder Brother everything I knew about the assassination attempt. I also told him about my meeting with Chiang in Chungking, emphasizing Chiang's threat against me, Mei-hua, and, by implication, the twins.

Sun-yu's face darkened. "I'm glad you're taking Chiang's threat seriously. The Little Bandit is not a man one should ever ignore."

Sun-yu asked me several questions. I answered those I could, but, in fact, I had to admit I did not yet know enough to answer others.

"I assume," Sun-yu said, "Madam Chiang did not come to Shanghai on her own initiative. She most likely — almost certainly — came here on Chiang's behalf."

I nodded.

"But was her trip made to meet with the enemy or was the trip arranged for her to meet with Chiang's KMT-Shanghai Resistance?"

"I assume she came to meet with the enemy. Otherwise, sending Madam Chiang here would be too risky. If Chiang just wanted to meet with his Resistance members, he could have sent someone expendable, some soldier or some diplomat."

I looked over at Eli. He was being unusually quiet.

He nodded. "That makes sense," he said.

I looked back at Sun-yu, and continued. "If Chiang just wanted to meet with his Shanghai Resistance, he could have summoned its leaders to Chungking, not risked sending the Dragon Lady into enemy-held territory to convey some message for him."

I looked from Elder Brother to Eli, but neither said anything, so I continued offering my own thoughts.

"What could Madam Chiang achieve by meeting with Chiang's Resistance in Shanghai that would be worth the risk to her of going there? Madam Chiang would be safe in enemy-held Shanghai only if she was here for a diplomatic meeting that had been prearranged with the Dwarf Bandits."

"I agree," Sun-yu said, "but what could the purpose of such a meeting be."

I shook my head. "I don't know. Chiang didn't tell me. But

if the mission concerned the enemy Dwarf Bandits, there are only so many possibilities."

Elder Brother nodded. "The mission might have been to negotiate the terms of the surrender of Chiang's army to the Dwarf Bandits on terms favorable to Chiang. As you know, Madam Chiang has often negotiated sensitive matters on her husband's behalf."

"I doubt that," I said. "I can't imagine any reason why Chiang, at this point in the war, would surrender his army to the Dwarf Bandits. I expect Chiang will fight his enemies to the death if it should come to that. He would have nothing to lose by doing so."

Elder Brother shrugged, but said nothing. He seemed to want to hear more.

Eli spoke for the first time. "Perhaps it was the other way around. Maybe Chiang was offering surrender terms to the Japanese," he said, "giving them an opportunity to surrender to him before he annihilates them. Based on his reputation, he's arrogant enough to believe he has the upper hand and to consider doing just that."

"That's unlikely," I said. "Chiang might be arrogant enough to do that, but why would the Kwantung even meet with the Dragon Lady to consider that? Why would they surrender? The Dwarf Bandits are well ensconced in Shanghai and in other coastal cities. Chiang's army will never be able to dislodge them. The Dwarf Bandits have no reason to give up."

"Perhaps, then, Chiang wants a cease fire so he can pursue some other goal — maybe free up his army to go after Mao and the CCP," Elder Brother said.

"Maybe that was what he wanted," I said, "but I doubt the Dwarf Bandits would allow him that breathing space. Why would the Dwarf Bandits help out Chiang rather than continue to fight him? They are gradually wearing down the KMT, and eventually will defeat Chiang's army. Why would they surrender their current advantage and give Chiang breathing space. I don't think they would.

"Besides," I said, "Chiang can win if he can gain time to replenish his men and his supplies. He and Mao are cooperating under the terms of the Xi'an Agreement. It is in both their interests to honor its terms, to eventually wear-out the enemy, and eventually drive the Dwarf Bandits out of China."

"Let's consider this from a different point of view," Sun-yu said.

I poured more wine, then looked expectantly at Elder Brother.

"Without regard to why Madam Chiang might have come to Shanghai, who would want her dead once she was here?"

I laughed. "Just about everyone who has ever met her," I said.

"The Dwarf Bandits," Elder Brother said, "would not have had to ambush her if they wanted her dead. They could have taken her prisoner when she showed up here — even if she was in Shanghai on some agreed-upon diplomatic mission. They could have killed her while she was here in their custody.

"They could declare her death — even if it resulted from their betrayal of their diplomatic agreement — as a casualty of war. What consequences could there be for them in wartime? What could Chiang do to them that he hasn't unsuccessfully been trying to do to them since 1937?"

"Are you suggesting then that the KMT-Shanghai Resistance tried to murder her?" I said.

"I'm just thinking out loud, Younger Brother. Nothing more."

"Why would Chiang's own Resistance members want her dead?" I said. "I doubt they even knew she'd be in Shanghai."

"I don't know," Elder Brother said. "I'm just turning over possibilities in my mind, questions you might want to investigate."

"You might be on to something," I said, "but something involving Mao, not the KMT Resistance. Maybe the ambush was set up by Mao's Shanghai Resistance to humiliate and anger Chiang. Mao is very strategic. Perhaps he has a longer view of the war and its aftermath that we haven't considered."

"Maybe," Elder Brother said, "but for now we have no way of knowing." He paused to pour the last of the Tiger Wine. "I will contact my comrades in the Green Gang, and report back to you as soon as I can."

Eli and I left *The Heavenly Palace* and walked toward the Garden Bridge to cross over the Whangpoo back to the Settlement.

While we stood halfway across the bridge at a Kwantung checkpoint having our ID cards examined — a mandatory routine at this place on the bridge — I saw the man in the black suit and black Fedora. As before, he stared intensely at me. This time, however, when I looked into his eyes, he did not look away.

Who is he? I wondered. *Why is he following me? Why did he hold my stare this time and not look away as he had before?*

"Don't turn around and look," I said to Eli, "but we're being followed."

I told Eli about my experience with the man the other day.

"Is he working for the Kwantung?" Eli said.

"I shrugged. "Who else would he be working for? Probably for that colonel who came to my office and ordered me not to leave the Settlement. Now, for sure, the colonel will know I disobeyed his order and came to Frenchtown. That does not look good for me."

CHAPTER 37

Mei-hua and Eli

Current week. Fourth week of June. Shanghai.

M EI-HUA, ELI, AND THE LEADER in the CCP's Resistance movement, Fang Chi, gathered in the basement of a potion shop located on Canton Road in the Settlement. The shop's retail business operated on the ground floor, offering Celestials homemade medicines, lucky charms, and various potions created from deer horns, frog feet, lucky crickets, bird beaks, and other animal parts it ground into fine powders.

"We are fully committed, Comrade," Mei-hua said. She looked first at Fang Chi, then at Eli, who said, "We are," as he nodded.

"Mei-hua," Fang Chi said, "I know you had training years ago using explosives so you and I will plant the bomb. We will have ten minutes to escape the explosion once the timer has been set.

"I know ten minutes is not much time to escape, and that unavoidable delays might occur endangering us, but that will be all the time we can allow ourselves if we are to be certain to achieve our mission.

"The last three bombs we set were discovered by the Dwarf

Bandits and defused before they exploded. We cannot have that happen again. This time, the school building must be destroyed while it still is filled with Kwantung using it as one of their barracks."

"I understand, Comrade. You and I will escape within ten minutes or we will die for our cause," Mei-hua said.

CHAPTER 38

Sun-jin

Current week. Fourth week of June. Shanghai.

NOTICED SOMETHING STRANGE OCCURRING AS I moved around the Settlement.

I first became aware of it while walking along the Bund when I stopped at a corner newspaper kiosk. I lifted a copy of the *Shanghai Times* to see if there was any news in it interesting enough to cause me to buy the paper. I quickly looked through all the pages.

This paper, like all published in Shanghai, was now controlled by the arm of the Kwantung that regulated propaganda.

As I paged through the paper, I noticed there no longer were satirical cartoons or vitriolic articles vilifying Chiang or the KMT. I also noticed that the number of adverse articles and cartoons relating to Mao and the CCP seemed to have increased to take up the slack.

That's strange, I thought. *It's almost as if the Kwantung has made a separate agreement with Chiang and the KMT, and has removed them from its usual propaganda barrages.*

I bought the paper and walked on. When I arrived at the

intersection of the Bund and Nanking Road, I stopped to watch two Kwantung soldiers across the street as they white-washed an anti-KMT poster that has been on the side of a building for months. They then pasted an anti-Mao poster over it.

What's going on here?

I kept my distance and watched. In addition to the one anti-Mao poster which now covered the KMT poster, they also pasted two more anti-Mao and two more anti-CCP posters on the wall alongside it.

I was anxious to complete my walk and return home to turn on the radio. On any typical day, every show was preceded and followed by anti-KMT and anti-CCP propaganda.

Would that pattern still be followed or would the propaganda now be directed only against Mao and the CCP?

I arrived home to have an early dinner with Mei-hua and the children.

I turned on the radio and listened to it as I did other things.

The pattern held.

Meanwhile, it was not all business for me. The twins needed their hair cut, so, after dinner, instead of reading them a story as I usually do, I spread out a blanket on the kitchen floor, placed Ji and Fen, one at a time, on a low stool, and cut their hair.

I gave Ji the traditional little boy's haircut, but, following Mei-hua's desire, cut Fen's hair in the new, short style that modern young women were wearing in Shanghai these days.

Bik sat on the floor watching us, wagging her tail when she caught me glancing over at her, as if she was waiting for her turn after I finished with the twins.

As I cleaned up afterward, Mei-hua came into the kitchen, opened the ice box, and took out two *Black Panda* beers.

"I'll be in the other room with these," she said, "whenever you're finished."

I finished cleaning up, joined the children in their bedroom, put them into their beds, covered them with thick wool blankets, and told them a brief story before turning out the light.

Then I joined Mei-hua. I told her about Eli's and my visit with Sun-yu. I also told her, for the first time, about the man in the black suit and black Fedora who I believed was following me.

"Perhaps it's time for you to rethink this investigation," she said.

"Rethink it?" I said, frowning as I did so. "I think about it all the time, yet I cannot come up with a meaningful way to proceed because of the Occupation and the limitations it imposes."

"That's not what I meant. I know it's on your mind all the time. I meant rethink it, as in, *should I really be doing this at all?*"

"I'm surprised to hear you say that. You know what's at stake for us. Chiang made that clear. You've acknowledged that yourself."

Mei-hua nodded. "I understand. My advice was logical, perhaps, but also not practical. You seem to be caught between the Kwantung and Chiang, with no way out. Could Chiang have been bluffing when he threatened you, trying to intimidate you into pursuing this dangerous investigation?"

"Chiang does not have a reputation for bluffing," I said.

"Nor does the Kwantung," Mei-hua added.

CHAPTER 39

Sun-jin

Current week. Fourth week of June. Shanghai.

THE NEXT DAY, AT SUN-YU'S request, Eli and I met with him at *The Heavenly Palace*. He had called me and said he had information for us. I wanted to hear this directly from his lips, not over the telephone, so we could safely discuss what he'd learned. The telephones, rumors said, were tapped by the Dwarf Bandits, and all calls were listened to and recorded by the secret police.

After we finished the ritually prescribed Taoist and Confucian greetings to show respect for each other, and had accepted Elder Brother's offer of drinks, he said, "My acquaintances in the Green Gang have given me information that might be useful to you."

I waited as I sipped wine from a newly opened bottle of *Tiger Wine*. Eli drank beer.

"I have been told that the attack was planned in Chungking, not in Shanghai."

"If this is true," I said, "that means the CCP's Shanghai Resistance probably was not involved."

Eli shook his head. "That's not necessarily true," he said.

"That information does not eliminate Mao or the CCP. The underground CCP in Chungking could have learned about Chiang's mission and could have planned the assassination from there, thinking Chiang himself would be in the convoy in Shanghai. Then, Mao's Resistance here in Shanghai could have carried out the plan."

"I doubt that Mao would ever believe that Chiang would secretly come to Shanghai under any circumstances," Sun-yu said. "Why would Chiang allow himself to be in a secret convoy in enemy territory? That would be too risky. If the Kwantung ignored any agreement they might have had with him, they then could have taken him prisoner."

Elder brother shook his head. "No, that's not it. Chiang has never had a reputation for risking his well-being under any circumstances. He's known to be a coward."

I shrugged. "Maybe so. Anyway, if Chiang himself came to Shanghai, or had even sent his wife here, it must have been for some very important purpose, one that would require a temporary cease-fire with the Dwarf Bandits.

"It would have to have been important enough for Chiang to risk his life or risk his wife's life by coming to Shanghai," I said. "It would have to have been important enough that someone back in Chungking would want to kill Chiang or his wife to defeat that mission."

"But Chiang," Eli said, "told you his wife was in the car. He did not say he also was there. At least you never told me he said that."

"He didn't. All his references were to the assassination attempt against his wife, not against him and his wife." I paused to consider the situation. "I don't know what I believe at the moment. Chiang's reputation for truth leaves much to be desired.

"Who do you think might be behind the plot?" I said, looking first at Sun-yu, then at Eli.

"I think the most likely candidates either are some of Chiang's generals or some Kwantung generals, officers who learned of the mission and sought to undermine or block it," Eli said.

I nodded. "That's a plausible hypothesis, one that makes sense for now."

"This could be the first step in an attempted coup against the generalissimo," Sun-yu said.

"If his generals were involved, I would say it was," Eli added. "But if the assassination attempt was made by Kwantung generals, then the motive likely was something else."

I considered this for a moment, then said, "This investigation is becoming more and more confused as we proceed."

CHAPTER 40

Sun-jin

Current week. Last day of June. Shanghai.

THE NEXT MORNING, WHEN I arrived at the office, Eli was already there. He looked up from his desk as I walked into his office to say hello. His eyes were red and swollen, his hair uncombed. His face was unshaven and deathly pale.

Before I could ask what was wrong, he said, "My father is dead. Murdered by a Kwantung soldier this morning just after breakfast."

"What? How—"

"When he entered his stall to begin his workday, he caught a Kwantung soldier in the store. He'd broken in and had smashed a display case. The looter was trying to steal jewelry. When my father confronted him, instead of running away, he shot my father in his chest."

Avram was buried the next morning, within twenty-four hours of his death, as was the Hebrews' custom, in Shanghai's only Jewish cemetery. Unlike we Celestials who mourn our dead while wearing white clothing, the Jews, like other Round-Eyes, all wore black to the funeral.

After the funeral, Mei-hua and I went to Eli's home to join him and his mother as Eli sat *Shiva*. The observance was underway when we arrived.

The *Shiva* ritual — which normally occurs after sundown, but which now took place in the afternoon because of curfew — was performed by Jewish male mourners on behalf of the deceased and was carried out to aid the bereaved as they moved through the process of grieving.

Ordinarily, seven male relatives of the deceased would gather to sit *Shiva* for seven evenings, taking turns, one each night, reciting a prayer for the dead known as the *Kaddish*. In place of Avram's seven male relatives, since none lived in occupied Shanghai other than Eli, Eli and six of his male friends (including me) would gather at Eli's home over each of the next seven afternoons to say *Kaddish* for Avram.

As was customary, mourners who visited the *Shiva* home poured water over their hands before they entered. All mirrors were covered. The front door was left unlocked so visitors could enter without knocking or ringing a doorbell.

At the end of the seventh day, Eli told me when he explained the *Shiva* ritual to me, those of us who had sat *Shiva* would go outside and walk around the block to symbolize our return to the regular world.

During this *Shiva* period, Mei-hua and other women, all acting in the Jewish tradition known as *seudat havra'ah — the meal of consolation* — brought a meal for everyone or sent gifts of food to Eli's home. The Hebrews' tradition discourages the sending of flowers or gifts other than food.

On the first afternoon of *Shiva*, after Mei-hua and I arrived at Eli's home, Mei-hua and I paid respects to Eli's mother. Then I walked up to Eli and placed my hand on his shoulder. His face was pale and puffy. He looked as if he had been the one who died.

"I will miss Avram," I said. "He was as good a friend to me as he was a good father to you. We both were blessed to have had him in our lives."

Eli nodded, but said nothing.

Eli had no immediate family, other than his mother, with whom to share his despair. His two sisters had emigrated to America in early 1941. They could not return to occupied Shanghai to mourn their father or to visit his gravesite because Japan and the United States were engaged in the Second World War. Eli was on his own in Shanghai, having sole responsibility now for himself and his mother.

Mei-hua walked over and joined us.

"Mei-hua and I, along with your mother, now are your family," I said. "You and your mother always are welcome in our home."

Mei-hua put her arm around Eli's shoulder and hugged him. "Yes, Eli, you and your mother are always welcome. You are our good friends and comrades," she said.

JULY 1945

CHAPTER 41

Sun-jin

The first week of July. Shanghai.

WAS PUZZLED BY, AND CURIOUS about, the increased Dwarf Bandits' propaganda against Mao and, seemingly, in favor of Chiang.

The radio confirmed the same pattern as the propaganda posters I'd seen. It suddenly was as if the Kwantung and the KMT were not at war with each another.

Why would the Kwantung shift their propaganda efforts away from Chiang and the KMT, and now direct it just at Mao and the CCP?

Was there something going on between Chiang and the Dwarf Bandits?

Although I did not know if this was so, it seemed logical and a possibility.

If I'm correct, could it be related to Madam Chiang's secret trip to Shanghai and to the attempt on her life?

I decided I would have to take some personal risk if I was going to answer this question and discover who had tried to kill Madam Chiang.

To do this, I would go to Sassoon House and try to meet

with the colonel who had come to my office the other day. I realized I likely would not be permitted to see him, and that I might even be arrested as an enemy spy, but I had to take that chance. I was at a dead end in my investigation. I had never even gotten started. While I had several theories concerning what might have happened and I had several possible, but theoretical suspects, I hadn't made any actual progress in finding answers I could give to Chiang. I had to move on and get some answers before he brought me to Chungking again.

First, however, to prepare for my visit, I would have to visit Elder Brother again.

"I can get you all those things right now, Younger Brother," Sun-yu said. "Please tell me why you want them. It sounds like you are putting together a package of *squeeze*. Am I correct?"

Because my hands were full when I left Elder Brother, I took a taxi from *The Heavenly Palace* to the Bund. Sassoon House is located behind that street, at the corner where the Bund intersects with Nanking Road. This is across the street from where I saw soldiers covering up one anti-KMT propaganda poster and putting up several anti-CCP posters.

The building in which Sassoon House was located had been constructed by Victor Sassoon in 1928. It offered two unrelated functions within the same structure: a luxury-hotel portion known as the Cathay Hotel; and, an office building component known as Sassoon House. When Victor Sassoon fled Shanghai for London in December 1941, the Kwantung took over the Cathay Hotel portion of the structure as living quarters for its officers, and occupied the Sassoon House section as its office headquarters.

I approached the Sassoon House entrance. Two soldiers stood sentry at the doorway. I was stopped, searched, and, with the help of a translator they summoned, was asked my business, before being admitted to the lobby. I explained I wanted to see one of their colonels, that I had business with him. I described him although I could not name him.

One of the guards knew which colonel I meant. He called the colonel's office. I was given permission to proceed. A guard walked behind me as I headed to the lift and then followed me to the colonel's office.

Another guard stood in the hallway by the office door. He searched me again before I was admitted.

The colonel sat behind a desk, smoking a cigarette when I entered. His eyes narrowed when he recognized me.

"*Hai!* Why are you here?" he said. He did not offer me a seat.

"I would like to speak with you about something," I said. "It concerns the investigation I'm involved in."

"Why should I care about that? Your business is no concern to me unless you have violated my order to stay within the Settlement or unless you have spied on the Kwantung. Have you disobeyed my order or are you a spy?"

I hesitated. *Had the man in the black Fedora reported my trip to Frenchtown?*

"No, sir, I have not left the Settlement and I'm not a spy. I've brought you some gifts to thank you in advance for the aid I hope you will give me today." I held up the package I carried.

The colonel sat up a little straighter. "Sit," he said, as he pointed to the chair I stood next to.

I sat, reached into the package I carried, and placed several boxes of razor blades, three cartons of cigarettes, and two pairs of nylons on the desk.

"These are for you as an advance token of my appreciation," I said. "There can be more where these came from if you'd like, Colonel."

I paused, then asked, "What did you say your name was?"

"I did not say, but my name is Hisoka. Colonel Hisoka."

He picked up the cartons of cigarettes and placed them in a desk drawer. Then he moved the other gifts there, too.

"Why are you here?" he said.

"I need your help. I told you I'm a PI. I have some questions concerning my investigation."

Hisoka frowned. He stared briefly at the lit end of his cigarette.

"Why would I help you?"

I nodded toward the drawer in which he had placed the *squeeze* I'd brought him. "There can be more, much more, if you want."

His eyes narrowed. He said nothing. His drew heavily on his cigarette and blew the smoke out toward the ceiling. He looked back at me.

"*Hai!* Not today. I have no time for you today. Come back in a few days, then we'll see. Perhaps then, perhaps not."

I nodded and stood up. "Thank you," I said.

As I turned to leave, he said, "I will expect more gifts when you return."

CHAPTER 42

Mei-hua

The first week of July. Shanghai.

THAT SAME NIGHT AS AVRAM's funeral, Mei-hua — but not Eli, who had dropped out of the sabotage mission — and three other members of the CCP's Shanghai Resistance, waited until 3:00 a.m., then met in a dense stand of rare huanghuali-wood trees along Chaplow Road in Hongkew. Each knew the others only by sight and only by their *noms de guerre*. One by one, as they arrived, they quietly acknowledged one another with a nod or a handshake.

"Comrade," Mei-hua said to the third man to arrive.

He nodded at her. "Greetings, Comrade Zan."

Each was dressed from head to foot in black. Mei-hua's hair was pinned up under a dark beret. The ID-card she carried, as required under the Occupation, named her as Zan Bao — Precious Willow. No one carried any other item that might name them by their real identities for fear of placing their families and friends in danger should they be correctly identified, arrested or killed.

The group's leader looked over his team, then said, "Let's

darken our faces and hands with this." He held up a small glass jar filled with a black cream.

They helped one another with the camouflage ointment.

When they finished, the leader said, "I will briefly review our mission in case anyone has any last-minute questions. Our task should be quick and easily performed if you follow my instructions."

He looked from face to face, pausing until each acknowledged his statement by nodding, as if he was individually warning them.

"The bomb is in this knapsack." He pointed to the drab green canvas bag on the ground by his feet.

"Three of us will enter the barracks ground. Xi," he said to one of the men, "you will hide near the fence we've breached to keep watch and warn us of any trouble you see."

He handed Xi a small portable field telephone, one of many such devices that the American general, the Round-Eyes officer known as Vinegar Joe Stillwell, had given the CCP Resistance on behalf of the Americans.

"Yung Xun," he said to the other man, "you will enter the grounds with me and will go to back of the school to keep watch there."

He handed Yung a field telephone.

"Zan Bao and I," he said, nodding at Mei-hua, "will place the bomb at the school and will set the timer. If all goes as planned, we will meet at the cut in the fence no later than ten minutes after we've entered. If not, you know what to do. Any questions?"

Two men and Mei-hua crawled through the cut in the fence.

Xi positioned himself at a different location in the same thicket of huanghuali trees where they had rendezvoused, so he could watch the surrounding area and still see the fence.

Xi could see the former China Inland Mission School, the building now being used by the Kwantung to house troops after the Kwantung drove out the clergy, educators, and students. He could see the location at the structure where the leader would place the explosives. He could not see his comrades as they left the fence and crossed the grounds.

Minutes passed.

Xi watched and waited.

More time passed.

All was quiet.

Mei-hua and her three companions were away from the barracks, just a few dozen yards beyond the cut in the fence, when the bomb exploded.

In the chaos that followed, with Kwantung troop trucks racing toward the damaged building, and armed, frightened, angry troops being placed at every street corner within a one-kilometer distance from the barracks, the four CCP Shanghai Resistance comrades split up. Each successfully went to his separate destination.

CHAPTER 43

Sun-jin and Mei-hua

The evening of the explosion. The first week of July. Shanghai.

THAT SAME NIGHT, THE CHILDREN were in their beds asleep when Mei-hua arrived home from her meeting. Before she'd left, at nearly 3:00 a.m., I had asked her why she and her CCP Resistance comrades didn't meet during the day so they would not violate the Dwarf Bandit's curfew and take on all the risk that this involved. She merely answered, "It's not convenient for everyone." I didn't believe her, did not believe that was the reason, but decided not to press the matter. I saw no point in angering her since the meeting was already scheduled.

I wasn't able to sleep while she was gone. I was too nervous about her being out after curfew, so I waited up for her to return. I was sitting at the kitchen table, an empty bottle of rice whisky in front of me. I held a half-full glass in my left hand.

I heard Mei-hua come through the door. I hurriedly swallowed the last of my drink, stood up, and rushed over to her. I hugged her and kissed the top of her head.

"I've been so worried. I heard an explosion. Tell me that

this wasn't you," I said, leaning away from Mei-hua so I could see her face.

She nodded. "It was us. We did it. I'm exhausted from tension. I would like to go to sleep. We can talk in the morning."

I wasn't happy about that, but I could see she was totally depleted, so I did not object.

I was worried about her and the toll her return to CCP activity might take on her. Now I was worried that she was engaging in activities for which she would be put to death if she was caught.

We dressed for bed.

As Mei-hua slipped out of her black outfit, she gasped.

"What's the matter?" I said.

"Oh, no," she said. "No, no, no, no!"

"What?" My back stiffened.

I watched her check her pants and shirt pockets.

"My ID, the fake ID-card, it's missing," she said. She looked at me. "What should I do? I can't go back out to look for it."

I thought how to answer this because I knew my answer would not be a good one for us, specifically not a good one for Mei-hua. My experience as a former cop told me where this could go.

Before I could speak, Mei-hua relaxed and said, "At least the card isn't in my name. If it's found, there won't be any record of Zan Bao, a name I made up. I'll be all right."

I could see her relax as she realized this. I paused before delivering the bad news to her.

"That depends," I said, "on whether or not the card is found."

She frowned, appearing confused. "Why? There is no one named Zan Bao, at least no one with a connection to me."

"Yes there is, in a manner of speaking," I said. "The Kwantung will connect you through your fingerprints on the ID-card. When the Kwantung or the police cannot locate anyone named Zan Bao, they will lift the prints off the card — your fingerprints, not anyone else's, and only your fingerprints. They will have you when they compare that specimen to the prints of everyone who registered with the police and received genuine identity papers — people like you and me."

Mui-hua's face fell. She began to tremble. I took her in my arms and held her tightly.

CHAPTER 44

Sun-jin and Eli

Shanghai. The morning after the explosion.

WHEN I LEFT HOME TO go to the office, I was exhausted from my night of drinking and little sleep as I waited for Mei-hua to return home. Mei-hua was still in bed asleep. She'd told me before we fell asleep that the *amah* would take the children to the Swift Deer park to play this morning and then would take them to Sun-yu's house to play with his children. Sun-yu's wife would return Fen and Ji to us the next day before curfew.

I was free to go to work. I went into the office to pick up the investigation's file to bring home. I didn't think I would accomplish much today at the office or out in the field. I was too tired.

Much to my surprise, Eli came into the office just after I arrived. He looked sad and confused. It was obvious that Avram's death was weighing heavily on him.

"You shouldn't be here," I said. "Take time off. Stay home. I'll handle the investigation."

"I'm not here to work. I want to talk to you before *Shiva* this afternoon."

We locked the office front door and sat on the sofa in the waiting room facing each other from opposite ends.

"I've lost my interest in working, at least for now. I have to figure out what I want to do with my life. Frankly, I don't care about Chiang and his investigation. I'm sorry that I'm probably disappointing you after all you've done for me, but I don't know if I even want to continue as a PI anymore or do something else."

I shrugged. "I understand. I find it hard to concentrate, too. I catch myself thinking about Avram when I should be focused on Chiang's case. But I think you shouldn't rush into a decision. Take as much time off as you need, then make a decision."

After Eli left, I went into my office. I was reviewing my case notes when I heard the office door open and close.

I walked to my doorway to see who had come in.

It was Eli again. *Had he changed his mind about working today?*

"I'm surprised to see you back here," I said. "Have you decided to work after all until *Shiva* later today?"

"No, my friend, I have not. I have no interest in work or in politics either. I won't be returning to work here and I am giving up the CCP."

Although I was happy Eli was leaving the CCP and all it represented, I was not happy he'd lost interest in work. I had assumed this feeling would pass with time.

"As I said before, you shouldn't make a decision right now," I said. "Take some time."

He shook his head. "I have already made a decision. Since I

have no family left here other than my mother, we've decided to move to the United States. My sisters are there — one in New York and one in Washington, DC."

That caught me off guard. "Isn't that pretty sudden, to move there? Our cultures are so different even though you originally were from the West."

"After I left here this morning, I went to see a friend of my father's. The man is a member of our refugee community. He also is a master forger. He will create exit and travel papers for my mother and me so we can leave Shanghai, travel to Singapore, and eventually make our way to neutral Lisbon. Our documents should be ready within a week."

I thought about what I wanted to say. I did not want him to think I didn't respect his decision and was trying to talk him out of it.

"All right. If your mind is made up, so be it. After *Shiva,* when it is appropriate again to do so, come have an early dinner with Mei—hua, me, and the twins. You can be home before curfew. I would like to hear your plans. Perhaps we can help you."

CHAPTER 45

Mei-hua

Shanghai. The morning after the explosion.

MEI-HUA AWOKE LATE IN THE morning as the *amah* nosily entered the apartment. She'd brought a few available groceries with her that she purchased on her way back from Sun-yu's home. Sun-jin, as he and Mei-hua planned, had already left for his office. They would meet this afternoon at Eli's home for the fourth day of *Shiva*.

Mei-hua was talking with the *amah* when suddenly the apartment door burst open.

Mei-hua and the old woman turned toward the door, their bodies rigid with fear. Mei-hua reflexively assumed a *Shaolin* defensive fighting posture. She relaxed her form when she saw four Kwantung troops, including one officer, enter the apartment, their weapons ready to fire. She would be no match for four men and four guns if she launched a *Shaolin* attack.

The brown-suited officer stormed over to Mei-hua. He drew his sword and raised the glistening blade toward her.

Mei-hua shuddered and took a step backward. "What is this?" she said. "How dare you—"

"Quiet," said the officer, speaking heavily accented Hu. "Do not say any more unless I ask you a question."

He nodded at the other soldiers. One pointed his rifle at Mai-hua and the *amah*. The other two left the room and searched the apartment. When they returned, they reported, speaking Japanese, that no one else was there.

"Show me your ID," the officer shouted at Mei-hua. He ignored the *amah*.

He examined the card, then said, "You will come with us." He nodded at one of the soldiers, who proceeded to bind Mei-hua's and the *amah*'s wrists behind their backs.

The *amah* softly cried as two soldiers led her away.

Mei-hua trembled. She could not control herself.

They were taken to Kwantung headquarters at Sassoon House. The women were separated from each other. Mei-hua would never see the *amah* again.

Mei-hua was brought to the office of a Kwantung major.

He sat behind a desk and motioned for Mei-hua to sit in the chair across from him. A soldier untied her wrists. The major offered Mei-hua a cigarette. She accepted.

After the major had leaned across the desk and had gallantly lit her cigarette, he sat back again, then said, speaking Hu, "You are in much trouble."

Mei-hua said nothing.

"We know you are a saboteur, Wu Mei-hua, that you are a member of the Communist underground and a Resistance member. We also know you blew up the barracks during the early morning. We have your fake ID-card. The penalty for sabotage is death."

CHAPTER 46

Sun-jin

The morning after the explosion. Shanghai.

A FTER I ARRIVED AT THE office, I changed my mind about how I would spend my day. I decided not to take the investigation file home to work. Instead, I would go see Colonel Hisoka. I would follow-up on my last visit when he did not have time to talk to me, but offered to allow me to return. I left my office and waited for the electric streetcar to arrive, but gave up after thirty minutes. Trolleys had become so unreliable, like so many aspects of our lives under the Occupation.

I saw a rickshaw approaching so I raised my arm and shouted, *wang-ba-tso! — yellow wagon!* —— the traditional gesture and phrase used to hail one. The rickshaw was pulled by a coolie who was dressed in a threadbare shirt, faded shorts, and a lady's straw hat with plastic flowers sticking out of the band. Typical dress for this class of street coolie.

I took the bone-jarring ride from the streetcar stop near my office to the colonel's office at Sassoon House.

When I arrived, I easily passed through the search of me and my knapsack conducted by one of the two sentries standing at the entryway to the building. An interpreter again was summoned. He called the colonel's office for me.

I rode the lift to the third floor, accompanied by a soldier, and stopped in front of Colonel Hisoka's office. I was searched again by a guard before being permitted to enter.

"Sit, Mr. Ling. I've been expecting you."

"I know you're busy, Colonel, so I'll come right to the point."

Hisoka leaned back in his chair and drew heavily on his cigarette. He nodded. "I also will come right to the point. Have you brought me more gifts?"

"I have." I reached into the knapsack I was holding and extracted three cartons of cigarettes and two bottles of whisky. I put them on the desk.

The colonel eyed them with satisfaction, smiling as he nodded. He placed them in a drawer before turning back to me.

"Go on," he said.

"I've noticed that your soldiers have been removing or covering-over posters that attack Chiang Kai-shek or the KMT. I've also noticed that your soldiers have been replacing them with anti-Mao or anti-CCP posters.

"It also seems to me that the Kwantung no longer attacks Generalissimo Chiang or the KMT on its radio broadcasts. Am I correct in all this or is this my imagination?"

"You are correct. That is a good observation by you."

"Can you tell me why you're doing this?" I said.

He shrugged. "We are following orders."

"Why would someone order that done with respect to its enemy in wartime?" I said.

Hisoka shrugged, drew heavily on his cigarette, and said, "It is just the way of war. Nothing special. One day, we likely will put up new anti-Chiang or anti-KMT posters and have new broadcasts that will laud Mao and the CCP in our messages."

"With all due respect to you, Colonel, I believe there is more to this than what you've said. For example, the newspapers have recently indicated that many Celestial civilians have been released from the city's eight internment camps. That couldn't be a coincidence."

Hisoka seemed to be thinking of a response as he stared at his burning cigarette.

"I will tell you this much," he said. "Some arrangement — I don't know its terms — has been made by the KMT and Kwantung. There definitely is a lull in our hostilities and in the propaganda we usually offer against Chiang, his government, and his army."

This information both shocked me, and yet did not. It was not unusual in war for opposing sides to call a temporary halt to hostilities while they tried to find a basis for peace — temporary or permanent — or while they regrouped before resuming combat. That was the Way of War according to Sun Tzu.

Was that what had occurred here? If so, could I take advantage of this lull in hostilities, as Chiang suggested, to conduct my investigation without the Kwantung's interference? I would ask.

"In that case, Colonel, will you permit me to conduct my investigation without interference by the Kwantung? May I now leave the Settlement to investigate?"

"Yes, but only to investigate, and only for so long as I believe you are not a spy taking advantage of the lull. And, of course, only so long as you continue to bring me gifts."

"I understand."

"Do you, Mr. Ling? I doubt it," he said.

That puzzled me. I must have frowned and looked confused because he continued his statement.

"My soldiers have reported to me that you defied my previous order and left the Settlement to go to Hongkew."

That surprised me, yet it did not. But his soldiers told him? Not the man in the black Fedora?

I now understood why I thought I was being followed although I did not see the Celestial in the black Fedora when I looked for him. The colonel obviously had both soldiers and a civilian following me.

CHAPTER 47

Mei-hua

Shanghai. The morning after the explosion.

MEI-HUA LOOKED AT THE KWANTUNG major sitting across from her at Sassoon House. He smirked at he watched her watch him.

She began a *Shaolin* breathing exercise to relax herself. She stared hard into the officer's eyes. He did not look away. Nor did she.

He knows he has me trapped, figured out, that cold bastard, she thought.

"*Ayeeyah!*" she said. "You know no such things about me because I am none of those things you accuse me of. I am merely a Celestial mother and wife who stays at home and tends to her family. Nothing else. I have nothing to do with the war or any explosion. You have confused me with someone else."

"I see," said the major. "And I suppose you've never heard of a woman named Zan Bao."

She shook her head. "I have no idea who you're talking about."

"And I suppose it is a coincidence that your fingerprints —

and only yours, not Zin Bao's or anyone else's — were found on Zin Bao's ID-card. How would that occur?

"As I said, we know you are a saboteur. We know Zan Bao's ID-card is a fake. We will execute you and your husband, and then we will send your children to Japan to be raised as servants," he said.

Mei-hua shuddered. "I am not what you think," she said. She strained to keep her voice calm. "I have no idea who that woman is you mentioned or why you think I am anything other than a caring wife and mother."

The major took a deep breath. "I see. In that case, I'll tell you what I believe I know about you."

He lit another cigarette, drew heavily on it as he arranged his thoughts. He leaned back in his chair.

"I believe you are a member of the Shanghai Resistance. Based on your history as a former CCP member, you likely are a member of the CCP's Shanghai Resistance, not the KMT's." He smirked at Mei-hua.

"How am I doing so far?" he said. He chuckled.

Mei-hua remained silent, breathing deeply, slowly, quietly.

"Your identity in the Resistance, your *nom de guerre*, is Zan Bao. It is her ID-card we found when we searched the area near the barracks.

"The card is a fake," the major said. "We checked on Zan Bao. There is no such person registered with the police. There are no fingerprints on file for any person named Zan Bao. But your fingerprints, of course, are on file, and they were the only ones found on the fake card.

"So, I ask you again, how do you explain that?"

CHAPTER 48

Mei-hua

Shanghai. The morning after the explosion.

EI-HUA FROZE INWARDLY WHEN THE Kwantung officer described the fingerprints found on the fake papers, but she maintained her inscrutable, outward composure.

He knows! she thought. *Just as Sun-jin said.*

"*Hai!*" the major said. "That's right. We checked your fingerprints against those we found on the false papers. You and Zan Bao are one and the same person."

He leaned back, away from his desk, his victory written all over his face.

"I am not that person," Mai-hua said. "I told you, I am merely a wife and—"

The officer slammed his palm on the desk, causing Mei-hua to flinch.

"Stop!" he shouted. "Stop right now. No more lies. You insult me with each lie you tell. I'm not a fool. You will tell me the truth now or I will arrest you. You will regret it if I do."

Mei-hua breathed shallowly, slowly, deliberately. She composed herself and slowly shook her head.

"I have told you the truth, Major. I just hadn't yet had a

reason to tell you entire truth, the circumstances surrounding that truth, because it had not yet come up. I see I was mistaken. I wrongly believed that the less I said, the more easily this unfortunate mistake would be cleared up so I could be released. Because I was mistaken, I will tell you those surrounding circumstances now.

"I found the ID-card lying on the ground two days ago when I was walking to the Golden Karp Market on Canton Road, near the mission school — I mean, near the barracks.

"I picked it up because I thought I had dropped my card. When I saw it was not mine, I placed it back on the ground and continued on to my shopping."

"Why would you return the card to the ground rather than keep it?" the major said.

"I thought it was wise not to keep it. I did not want two sets of IDs on me if I was subject to a routine stop by your soldiers. I was afraid they would not believe me when I told them I'd just found Zan Bao's ID-card. The penalty for carrying false papers, as you know, is death."

"And why didn't you tell me before this?"

"I was afraid you wouldn't believe me if I told you the entire truth. It was such a strange coincidence."

The major considered her answer. She'd been right. He did not believe her.

This woman is smart, he thought. *She has prepared her answers for every question. I should just arrest her, have her interned, questioned, and shot. I would not need to worry then if she is being truthful.*

He considered this. *Yet she might still be useful to me. If I execute her now, I might miss the chance to have her watched and to learn more about her Resistance group. I can always arrest her later. I will not need any reason for that. So, for now, I will play her game.*

I will not continue to ask her the obvious question — why her fingerprints were the only ones on the false papers, why Zan Bao's prints were missing from the ID-card if Zan Bao and she are two different people? That question and her inability to answer it would force me to arrest her. That would not be the best course for now, would not bring me the information I want.

The major leaned back in his chair. "I see," he said. "You expect me to believe your fanciful, convenient story? My ten-year-old daughter tells lies better than you do."

"Believe what you want, sir. It is not a story. It is true," Mei-hua said. Her voice now reflected newly found confidence. The officer seemed to be considering her situation, not merely threatening her as before.

"You are fortunate," the major said, "that you have young children, fortunate also that I also am a loving parent, and lucky, too, that I am a sympathetic person who prefers not to harm a young child's mother.

"Your story has just enough plausibility that I will give you the benefit of the doubt. This time. But be careful, Wu Mei-hua," he said, as he stood up. You will not have another chance."

And you better lead me to your saboteur colleagues before too long or I might change my mind and arrest you and your husband without waiting.

CHAPTER 49

Sun-jin

Shanghai. The evening after the explosion.

MEI-HUA AND I WERE SITTING in the kitchen drinking *baijiu*, a sorghum-based whisky. We were talking about her interrogation by the Dwarf-Bandit major earlier in the day.

I repeatedly rubbed the back of my neck, which felt stiff and sore from tension. Mei-hua bit her lower lip. We were nervous about her near-arrest experience and by the narrow escape it represented. I decided not to remind her that I had asked her not to participate in any way with the CCP, obviously not take part in sabotage. In just the thirty minutes we'd been sitting, we had almost emptied the full bottle of whisky.

There was a knock on the door — actually it was a police-style pounding on the door, the type of pounding I employed years ago when I still was an inspector-detective, and we were raiding a home or business.

We looked at each another, tension and fear obvious on the other's face. I abruptly stood. I held up my palm and shook my head to indicate that I would like Mei-hua to remain in the kitchen.

When I opened the door, three Celestials dressed as Dwarf-Bandit soldiers pushed their way past me into the living room.

They've figured out the fake ID-card belonged to Mei-hua. They've come for her. Now she — probably me, too — will not escape hanging or a firing squad.

I froze.

I glanced behind me. Mei-hua, stood in the doorway between the kitchen and the living room. She stared at the soldiers, one hand partially covering her mouth. Her face had lost its color.

The soldiers ignored Mei-hua. They faced me.

"We know who you are," the soldier said to me, speaking a poor version of Hu, "so you will please come with us." His accent was Cantonese.

I was surprised he was looking at me and ignoring Mei-hua whose presence was apparent. And, not only that, he'd said *please*.

"We have been ordered to bring you to the generalissimo. We will return you here tomorrow."

"You're not Kwantung?" I said. "But your uniforms are those of—"

"We must hurry," he said, motioning me toward the door. "Come now. There is no time to waste. There is a plane waiting for you."

Generalissimo Chiang was not pleased to see me even though he had arranged to bring me to Chungking.

"Your time is running out," he said. "I want the names of the people who plotted my wife's death, and I want those names soon. Are you willing to delay resolving this and cost your wife and your loved ones their lives?"

"I'm doing the best I can under the circumstances, sir. Occupied cities aren't designed to make investigations easy."

"That's not an acceptable excuse," Chiang said.

"Perhaps, sir, if you will tell me the nature of the mission your wife was pursuing in enemy-occupied Shanghai, I might use that information to narrow and focus my investigation."

"You have no need to know that."

This was not going well, and I had no idea how to improve it.

"I can tell you this, Generalissimo. I have learned that the plot originated in Chungking, not in Shanghai, so you need to look among your own contacts here, even as I continue to investigate in Shanghai."

Chiang frowned. He lit a cigarette, blew smoke toward the ceiling, looked back at me, then said, "How do you know that?"

"I was told by my contacts in the Green Gang," I said. "I also should tell you that some Celestial collaborator has been following me. I'm concerned I'm going to be arrested and will not be able to complete my investigation for you."

Chiang smiled. "You will not be arrested by him or by the Kwantung as long as you are not obvious about the investigation. The man following you is not a collaborator. He is one of my agents in Shanghai. He reports to me on your activities.

"And," he added, "if you do not rub their noses in shit, the Kwantung will not interfere with your investigation. They have reasons to cooperate."

"Why would they—"

He dismissed my question with a flick of his hand. "You do not need to know why," he said, "but you must wrap-up this investigation within the next day or two at the latest. That is my order. I will not tolerate your continued delay and insubordination."

I had no answer for that so I changed the subject to another important question I had.

"One more thing, Generalissimo."

He frowned. "Go on."

"I've noticed recently that the Dwarf Bandits in Shanghai have changed their propaganda to eliminate you and the KMT from it. Now, their negative propaganda all is focused on Mao and the CCP. Do you know why that would be? It seems strange."

Chiang smiled, exposing his stained teeth. "There is no need for you to know that. Take advantage of this situation and complete your investigation while you may still move around the city."

He called in the guard.

I was back in Shanghai eight hours later. I noticed for the first time that the Kwantung at Shanghai's airport did not treat the Celestials accompanying me as their enemy, that they were respectful of them.

CHAPTER 50

Sun-jin

Shanghai. Two days after the explosion.

FTER *SHIVA* ENDED AND ELI was free again to resume his customary life, Eli arrived for dinner at 2:00 p.m., the early hour having been chosen to avoid a curfew problem. He brought one set of wooden toy blocks for Fen and another set for Ji. Neither set looked new, and probably had been purchased by Eli on the black market at great expense.

He looked slightly better than he'd seemed the last time I saw him. Perhaps the decision he made to leave Shanghai and move to the United States had provided him with some relief, some escape from his grief for Avram. I would miss him.

After he and Mei-hua hugged, we sat to have drinks and talk. Since Eli did not like *Tiger Wine*, we skipped that. Instead, Mei-hua opened a bottle of *Yunnan Red* and served it.

"Are you firm in your decision to leave Shanghai?" I said.

"It's for the best. My mother and I will spend time with both my sisters. My mother then will move to New York. She will live with my sister and her family. I'll decide in which city I want to live to be near one of them. I suspect that it will be

Washington, DC, not New York, since I am closest to my sister who lives in Washington with her husband and children.

"I will live in that city's Chinatown since, oddly enough, even though I am European, I now am more comfortable living and working among Celestials than I am living and working among Occidentals.

Mei-hua called us in for dinner. She served beef thigh, marinated in lemon juice, one of Eli's favorite meals. This had cost us most of our food-ration coupons for the month, but she and I had talked about this and had decided that this meal was a fitting occasion for such a luxury. Mei-hua found the meat on the black market. We would make it through the balance of the month with help from Elder Brother. I had already spoken to him about it.

Everyone, including the twins, who seemed to sense that something final and sad was occurring, remained subdued throughout the meal.

CHAPTER 51

Sun-jin

Shanghai. Two days after the explosion.

THAT SAME EVENING, LONG AFTER Eli had left and the children and Bik were asleep, and while Mei-hua sat at the kitchen table and read this week's issue of the revitalized Communist newspaper, *Slovo*, I lit a cigarette, poured a *Clover* beer, and thought about the next step in my investigation.

I knew I would have to be creative because the time for wrapping this up was coming to an end. Chiang had made that clear. I would have to deliver results to him in the next day or two, or would have to face whatever consequences he might dole out to me and my family. I didn't care to consider that possibility.

I thought about my recent meeting with Chiang. It struck me at that time that he did not seem surprised when I mentioned that the Kwantung had started removing anti-Chiang and anti-KMT propaganda from telephone posts, fences, walls, and from the radio airwaves, replacing them with much more anti-CCP and anti-Mao propaganda than before.

Was it possible that Chiang and the Kwantung had made some arrangement that was secret, and that Chiang and the Kwantung were now allies? Was that why Madam Chiang had been in Shanghai, to make that arrangement for Chiang?

Was that also why Chiang said I should take advantage of the propaganda lull to investigate the plot against his wife, saying that the Kwantung would not interfere with me?

Had he been hinting that I could — or that I should — look for help or, at least, look for passive acceptance from the Kwantung? If not that, what else could he have meant?

I thought about this. As unlikely as it should be, it seemed Chiang and the Kwantung did have some sort of quiet arrangement. They must have.

Should I explore the possibility of my hunch or would I place myself in danger by doing so?

Would I be wasting valuable time doing so?

What if I relied on this, but was wrong? That would cost me valuable time. If I failed to deliver an answer to him in the next day or two, Chiang would not be forgiving.

But what other choice did I have since my investigation had stalled and my time was running out?

I decided I would rely on this hypothesis.

I decided to again visit Kwantung Colonel Hisoka at Sassoon House to ask for his help.

CHAPTER 52

Sun-jin

Shanghai. Two days after the explosion.

THE INFORMATION I HAD LEARNED from Colonel Hisoka in my previous visit to him puzzled me, but he'd had no reason to mislead me. If he had not wanted me to know it, he could have refused to tell me anything.

Although his information was confusing as to the Dwarf Bandits' motive, Hisoka's statements appeared to be plausible. It seemed that some sort of truce or cessation of hostilities must have been arranged between the KMT and the Kwantung, and that now — at least for the time being — the Kwantung was directing its hostile propaganda in Shanghai, and perhaps in all of China, only against the CCP and Mao.

I thought about this.

Why would the KMT and Kwantung enter into a secret truce?

Why would the Kwantung now direct its propaganda only against Mao and the CCP? Was that part of the truce agreement?

Was the Kwantung still engaged in hostilities with the CCP? With the KMT? If 'yes' with regard to the KMT, then my hypothesis that there was a truce would be wrong.

I also thought about Madam Chiang's brief presence here

in enemy-occupied Shanghai. I couldn't think of any reason she would have come here unless her presence was connected to something as significant as a truce and an intended cease fire.

The more I thought about this, the more I was convinced her presence had to be related to a truce. She had, after all, previously demonstrated her ability to bring about temporary peace between warring factions. She had negotiated a truce in 1936 between the KMT and the CCP — the Xi'an Agreement — so each army could expend all its efforts and resources against the enemy Dwarf Bandits, rather than dissipate their resources and strength fighting each another.

So what, then, was the connection between a truce, Madam Chiang's presence in Shanghai, and the attempted assassination of Madam Chiang?

I could think of only one logical connection that might cause an attempt on her life. Someone wanted to prevent the occurrence of a truce by killing Madam Chiang in enemy territory. Perhaps that person expected that her death there would so anger Chiang that he would blame the Kwantung for her assassination, and that Chiang then would cancel the truce agreement.

PART FOUR

CHAPTER 53

Sun-jin

Shanghai. Two days after the explosion.

ASSUMING MY HYPOTHESIS WAS CORRECT, *who would want to prevent a truce? Who might want to do that so very much that he would be willing to kill Chiang's wife, to commit treason to undermine Chiang's plan?*

Would Mao and the CCP want to block the truce? Of course they would. They would not want all the Kwantung's might directed solely at them rather than, as before a truce, diluted between the CCP and the KMT?

But did Mao even know about Madam Chiang's mission? There was no way for me to find out.

Who else might want to block a truce?

Although I ruled out Chiang himself since he obviously wanted the truce to occur, I decided Chiang's generals were likely candidates to undermine Chiang's plan. If they could convince Chiang that the Kwantung had betrayed him by trying to kill Madam Chiang when she was in Shanghai on a peace mission, how hard would it be for them to convince Chiang that he should not enter into a treaty with the duplicitous Dwarf Bandits? Not hard at all, I assumed.

But would Chiang's generals dare attempt this?

I doubted it. Such an act would be treason, and the penalty for treason was death. Chiang's generals did not have reputations for patriotism, bravery, or self-sacrifice. They were survivors of Chiang's many purges of his officers' corps, survivors because they had consistently been passive and had supported Chiang, the primary conditions for survival under Chiang's leadership. Those who had survived did not raise questions about Chiang's judgment or decisions.

In any event, the generals were not my problem because they were in Chungking. Chiang had made it clear in our first meeting that Big-Eared Tu would see to the Chungking investigation. My concern was to be with Shanghai.

Since Chiang wanted the investigation to continue, I assumed Tu had not uncovered a role in the plot by Chiang's generals.

If not the generals, then who else? I wondered.

Perhaps some civilian close to Chiang.

I also couldn't rule out that someone on the Kwantung's side might have been responsible for the assassination attempt. Perhaps a Dwarf- Bandit general or some civilian high in the Dwarf Bandits' government who opposed the making of the treaty?

This seemed just as likely or, at least, just as reasonable as pointing my finger at Chiang's generals. The problem, of course, was that I could no more investigate the Kwangtung's generals or a highly placed Dwarf-Bandit civilian than I could investigate Chiang's generals who are in Chungking. All these groups were off-limits to me.

I decided to focus my attention on the other people who are close to Chiang, people who might have a reason to assassinate Madam Chiang in order to block the truce.

CHAPTER 54

Sun-jin

Shanghai. Two days after the explosion.

B EFORE THE OCCUPATION, AT THIS point in any investigation, I normally would have ridden a Yellow-Swallow taxicab from my office to the public library to begin the task of paging through back copies of Shanghai's, and some other cities' newspapers — the *North-China Daily News*, the *Shanghai Times*, the *Peking Grey Lizard*, the *North China Star*, and the *Canton Daily Flower,* among others. I would be checking to see if recently reported battles with the Kwantung involved only the CCP or if they also involved the KMT. This would have tested my hypothesis.

But these were not normal times. I could not go to the library under the Occupation. One of the first actions taken by the Kwantung when they marched into the Settlement was to close all public buildings, including the library.

To test my hypothesis that the KMT and Kwantung were no longer engaged in hostilities, I would have to gain access to these newspapers from some other source, some other library in some unoccupied city.

I knew how to achieve this, but wished I did not have to resort to it.

When the Dwarf Bandits took over Shanghai, those newspapers that did not shut down permanently moved their operations to other cities in unoccupied China. Most went to Chungking with Chiang and his government so they could be close to the main source of most news.

I would have to have someone perform research for me about recent battles in those exiled newspapers. For that, I would have to turn to Mei-hua — reluctantly, of course, given the nature of the request I would make. I would ask her to have one of her undercover CCP colleagues in Chungking research the battles to see if my hypothesis was correct.

I telephoned Mei-hua and explained the situation to her. There was a brief moment of silence on her end of the call. I could see her grinning. Then she returned to the telephone.

"Of course I'll do this for you," she said. "I will turn right to it. I know someone who works in the library in Chungking. It might take a few hours or so."

As I hung up the telephone I realized that Mei-hua, when she heard my request, hadn't gloated, hadn't even reminded me that I was calling upon her CCP resources for help. I loved that woman.

I turned to other aspects of the investigation as I waited for Mei-hua to get back to me.

Mei-hua called me several hours later.

My hypothesis proved correct. While few battles were reported at all because no reporter was likely present when they occurred, the several that were reported over the past week involved only the CCP and the Kwantung. There was none reported involving the KMT and the Kwantung.

My hypothesis of a truce existing between Chiang and the Kwantung seemed correct.

CHAPTER 55

Shanghai. Two days after the explosion.

WHILE I WAS WAITING FOR Mei-hua to call me with the results of the research, I had called the informants I hadn't been able to contact before. Again, I did not reach any of them.

Next, I made a list of everyone publicly known to be close to Generalissimo Chiang. There were only a few people — his wife, his brother-in-law, and Big-Eared Tu.

I eliminated Madam Chiang for the obvious reason she would not have tried to have herself assassinated — that is, if the assassination attempt had been genuine, not a ruse by Madam Chiang to achieve some purpose I was not aware of. I had no way of knowing this, so I filed the possibility away for now. I would consider it again after I considered the other people possibly involved.

I eliminated Tu because he would not have had to have Madam Chiang killed if he wanted to block the truce. Tu was powerful enough that he could have just vetoed the treaty if he had wanted to put a stop to it. Even Generalissimo Chiang deferred to Tu's wishes when Tu made them known.

That left only Chiang's brother-in-law, T.V. Soong.

I knew about Soong as a general matter — that he was called a financial genius, that he was very close to his sister, and that he had saved the KMT and the Republic in the late 1930s by curbing hyper-inflation — at least until the war started and inflation returned. He was said to be very close to Chiang, one of his most trusted advisors. He also was an outspoken enemy of Mao and the CCP.

I went to visit Eli at his home. Unlikely as it might seem, since his father had been a businessman himself, Avram had been fascinated — probably obsessed was a better description — by T.V.'s life and career as a very successful businessman and financier. Avram had kept all manner of books, photographs, and articles (the latter two groups all carefully pasted into a scrapbook) relating to T.V. In fact, Avram, given the chance, could talk endlessly about the life, successes, and exploits of T.V. Soong, and his many and varied achievements over the years.

After Eli and I had a drink and lit cigarettes, I explained what I needed. We settled into his father's small office. Eli fetched all of Avram's books and five scrapbooks concerning T.V. He left me alone to go through them.

I confirmed, based on many articles, much of what I already knew from general gossip in Shanghai — that T.V. was a successful capitalist who openly detested Mao, the CCP, and the Communist economic system they represented. It appeared he apparently was willing to talk about that subject with any reporter who was interested. The scrapbooks were filled with such articles.

If this was so, I thought, *wouldn't Soong want the Kwangtung to assert all of its might against the CCP, as it seemed to be doing recently, rather than dilute its forces by fighting both the CCP and the KMT?*

Wouldn't the Kwantung be more likely to destroy Mao and the CCP if it could ignore Chiang and the KMT for the time being? Shouldn't this be what Soong would want?

If so, I thought, *perhaps T.V. would be satisfied with a truce that pitted the Kwantung against the CCP, but not against the KMT.*

It would seem so. At least on the face of this reasoning.

But I also learned from the scrapbooks that T.V. hated the Dwarf Bandits, hated them as invaders and occupiers of China, even more than he despised the Communists.

There was personal history here.

In 1931, after the Dwarf Bandits invaded and occupied Manchuria, creating the Mukden Incident to justify the invasion, T.V., still a young man, had publicly spoken out against the Dwarf Bandits at mass rallies of university students held that year in Shanghai, Canton, and Peking. Soong, the newspapers reported, had even been confined to jail for a short time by his own government just to appease the Japanese.

That would give him a reason to attempt to interfere with the truce. He would want the Dwarf Bandits driven out of China, using the combined power of the KMT and CCP, before Chiang turned against the CCP. Wasn't that the whole purpose of the Xi'an Agreement he and his sister had negotiated in 1936?

This made sense, and since everyone else close to Chiang had been eliminated — I had decided it was very unlikely Madam Chiang had staged her own assassination attempt in enemy-held territory — that meant T.V. Soong was the only possible person left.

But would Soong be willing to kill his sister to block a truce?

Not likely, I thought. The scrapbooks also made it clear that Soong and Madam Chiang were very close.

Would he sacrifice his beloved sister for the good of the country?

I doubted it. He likely arranged to have the attackers avoid her vehicle, but try to make it seem that she was the target so that Chiang, furious that someone had attempted to kill his wife in enemy-held Shanghai, would blame the Kwantung and would walk away from the truce before it was implemented.

There was no other possibility based on what I'd learned.

I was satisfied with my reasoning. It no longer seemed to be just a hypothesis. I believed I had completed my investigation.

Now I had to report this to Chiang and to convince him that I had figured out the plot. I had to see him again.

But would he believe me? Not likely. Not at first. I would have to convince him. If I failed, I probably would die at Chiang's hands.

CHAPTER 56

Sun-jin

Shanghai. Two days after the explosion.

I NOW HAD TO MAKE ARRANGEMENTS to again meet with Chiang.

I left my office and walked toward the Public Garden across the Whangpoo from Frenchtown.

It did not take long before I saw Chiang's man in the black suit and black Fedora following me.

I stepped into an alley, making sure he saw me do so, and waited.

I hid behind a pile of wooden barrels, about three meters into the alley.

When the man entered the alley looking for me, I stepped out behind him, blocking his way out.

"Ayeeyah," I said to get his attention. "We need to talk."

He was startled and spun around to face me. As he did so, he reached inside his suit jacket and pulled out a revolver. He pointed the gun at my chest.

I slowly raised my hands above my head, and said, "*Qing* — *Please.* I have an important message for Generalissimo Chiang.

I need to see him as soon as possible. Tell him I have completed my investigation for him."

The man frowned. His thick eyebrows came together.

"*Qivng rang? — What's that?*" the man said. "I don't know what you're talking about."

I nodded. "Just get my message to the generalissimo as quickly as possible if you want to survive this," I said. "He will not be happy with you if you fail to do that for him."

I slowly lowered my hands, turned away, and walked out of the alley. I assumed he would not shoot me in the back since there would be no way to justify that to Chiang. I clearly was not a threat to the man in the black Fedora.

Now I would wait for Chiang's undercover Celestials in Shanghai to come fetch me.

CHAPTER 57

Generalissimo Chiang

Chungking. Three days after the explosion.

I WAS SHOWN INTO CHIANG'S OFFICE the next morning after a flight to Chungking that lasted most of the night.

Madam Chiang was there, sitting on a sofa off to the side of the room. She ignored me as I entered Chiang's office and then stood, as directed, across Chiang's desk from him.

Chiang was smoking. He looked up and frowned as I was ushered in. He did not greet me at all.

"Who is the traitor?" he said. "What scum tried to murder my wife?"

"T.V. Soong."

I watched Chiang's face and neck darken. He became rigid before my eyes.

From the corner of my eyes, I could see Madam Chiang also stiffen. She looked over at Chiang, then, for the first time, looked at me. She remained silent. She glared at me with fire in her eyes.

"That's ridiculous," Chiang said. "Soong is loyal to me. He loves my wife and loves our country. He is a patriot."

I took Chiang through my reasoning, eliminating Mao and the CCP, as well as Madam Chiang herself.

I watched Chiang consider what I said, although he never acknowledged that he thought I might be correct. His face and neck remained dark. He finished one cigarette and started another as I stood there.

When I finished my explanation, Madam Chiang stood up and looked briefly at Chiang. She nodded once toward him, then left the office, still not acknowledging my presence. I had no idea if she believed me or not.

When we were alone, Chiang crushed out his cigarette, and said, "Have you eliminated everyone else?"

"Not quite, but I've eliminated everyone I could. I could not investigate the Dwarf-Bandit generals so it's possible one or more of them also might have been involved.

"Moreover, you told me not to investigate your generals, that Big-Eared Tu would take care of that. I assume Tu concluded your generals were not involved or you would not have had me continue my investigation. I have eliminated everyone close to you except Soong."

"You have done well, Mr. Ling. Now I have another order for you." He lit another cigarette, drew heavily on it, blew out the smoke, then looked hard in my eyes.

"This will remain between us. You will never speak of it to anyone else. No one at all. Understand?"

"Yes, sir."

"If I ever learn that you have disobeyed my order, you and your family will suffer."

"I understand."

"You are finished now. I will have you flown back to Shanghai."

CHAPTER 58

Generalissimo Chiang

Chungking. Four days after the explosion.

CHIANG SUMMONED T.V. SOONG TO his office.

He initially was cordial when his brother-in-law arrived. They settled at opposite ends of the sofa and faced each other. Chiang smoked his usual cigarette. Soong smoked a Dunhill cigar he'd brought with him, taken from a box he'd received from the American Round-Eyes aviator who led the ferocious Flying Tigers air squadron in China, Major-General Claire Chennault.

"*Ayeeyah!* Chiang said. "I know you were involved in the attempt on Mei-ling's life. Don't deny it. I can have you shot for treason."

T.V.'s face darkened. "*Shi — Yes,* I know you're able to do that, brother-in-law, but why would you? That would be very ill-considered, and it would do you no good. I have contributed much to the Republic and, specifically, to you. I intend to contribute more after the war if China survives.

"As for my sister, you know I adore her. I would never allow her to be injured or killed. My men were instructed that Mei-ling was not to be harmed. And she was not, was she?

Unfortunately, there was no way to prevent her from being frightened and angry."

"*Maskee — So you say,*" Chiang said. "Why did you do this? You know you now are a traitor to the Republic."

"Not so. I did this *for* the Republic, not to harm it. It is essential we drive the Dwarf Bandits from China before we destroy Mao and the CCP. That was the whole point and wisdom of the Xi'an Agreement. If we fail to drive out the Dwarf Bandits, it won't matter that Mao and the CCP exist. There will be no China for you to unify and rule."

"I can have you shot for your treachery. I *will* have you shot."

"Yes, you certainly can do that. That clearly is within your power, brother-in-law. But you won't do it. What could it possibly achieve for you other than to make you briefly feel good?"

Soong looked down and studied his cigar for a few seconds to let his statement take hold in Chiang's mind, then he looked back at Chiang.

"You are a pragmatic man, brother-in-law. That has been the basis for your success and survival over the years. You know that I am much more useful to you alive than I would be dead. Even in your anger, you must recognize that."

Chiang looked away and lit another cigarette. He stood up, walked over to his desk and sat down.

"The truce with the Dwarf Bandits is in effect now," Chiang said. "Your cowardly mission failed. There have been no recent battles between the KMT and the Dwarf Bandits. And all the Dwarf Bandits' forces are being thrown against Mao in the western provinces.

"Even as we assemble our troops in the east to attack Mao,

the Kwantung attack him from the west, just as we agreed. Like a giant python, we will squeeze Mao and the CCP to death between us."

"Let us hope, then, that the truce holds," T.V. said, "and that Mao is destroyed by the Kwantung. Unfortunately, I have no such expectation of that happening."

CHAPTER 59

Sun-jin

Shanghai. Five days after the explosion.

RETURNED HOME FROM CHUNGKING JUST after sunrise. I was exhausted, but wanted to talk to Mei-hua as soon as possible. I had much to tell her.

I woke Mei-hua and explained that I had just returned from Chungking. She made tea for us. We sat at the kitchen table.

"It is ended. The investigation is over," I said. "I have told Chiang that T. V. Soong was the person behind the assassination attempt."

Mei-hua frowned, then slowly smiled. "His brother-in-law?" She shook her head. "I would not want to be T.V. Soong if Chiang believed you."

"I think he believed me. I explained to Chiang how I had reached that conclusion, how I had eliminated all other possibilities. My accusation made logical sense. I don't think I would be home today if he hadn't believed me."

Mei-hua's forehead scrunched up. "Now what?" she said.

"Chiang told me I have finished my investigation and could go home. He also ordered me never to speak to anyone concerning this. He threated us again if I disobeyed his order."

"*Hao! — Good!*" Mae-hua said. "Now we can proceed with our own lives."

"We can only hope so," I said.

CHAPTER 60

Shanghai. Late September 1945.

THE SECOND WORLD WAR — including its subsumed Second Sino-Japanese War in China — officially ended when the Japanese signed the surrender document in Tokyo Bay on the deck of the USS *Missouri* on September 2, 1945.

But the expected peace the Japanese surrender offered China did not materialize. The end of Japan's occupation was not peace at all.

At first, after Japan's surrender, Chiang's KMT army temporarily occupied Shanghai. Yet the defeated Japanese, with Chiang's consent, continued to play a part in the day-to-day life of the city.

Because Chiang and his American colleagues preferred to have the Japanese maintain civil order in Shanghai, rather than give Mao an excuse to enter the city to bring about order and thereby oppose Chiang, they decided not to disarm the Japanese soldiers. Armed Kwantung, still patrolled Shanghai. Chiang even went so far as to order the Kwantung to keep fighting the People's Liberation Army in the rural provinces of China.

Shanghainese residents — especially high school and university students — were furious that the same Japanese soldiers — more than 100,000 of them — who had cruelly occupied Shanghai for eight years continued to patrol its streets and govern the city after their surrender in Tokyo Bay.

Each day, incensed high school and college-age students gathered to read the news posted on bulletin boards throughout Shanghai. It reported that Japanese troops still were fighting against Chinese — albeit, Chinese Communists — on direct orders from Chiang and the Americans. This did not endear the Nationalists or the Americans to the students.

Eventually, the Americans stepped in. American GIs began arriving in Shanghai to disarm and demobilize the Japanese. Chiang's troops returned from the provinces and took up posts in the city. Mao had been kept out of Shanghai.

But this would not last.

And there still was the matter of the Xi'an Agreement.

By its terms, the 1936 truce between Chiang and Mao — what was left of it, as a practical matter — automatically expired with the surrender of Japan on September 2.

The postponed Chinese Civil War resumed.

It raged throughout China.

Both Chinese sides fought once again to unify and control the country.

Life in Shanghai changed after Japan's surrender.

Now, in place of the swastika and the rising sun, the Nationalists and American flags flew over many streets. Giant portraits of Chiang lined Nanking Road and other strategic points around the city.

The foreign treaty concessions — the International Settlement and the French Concession — which had been informally, but futilely, ceded back to China in 1943 by the absent British, United States, and French as good-will gestures, now were officially returned to the Nationalists under formal treaties. The concessions now were referred to as the "former International Settlement" or the "former French Concession." Street names were changed to reflect this new, modern perspective.

Life in Shanghai went on, even as Mao and the CCP steadily fought their way toward the city.

EPILOGUE

1948 - 1949

CHAPTER 61

The City

S HANGHAI — FOR DECADES KNOWN AS the Whore of the Orient — the city where the Communist Party had been founded in 1921, represented great symbolic and historic importance to the Communists. The CCP intended to fully occupy Shanghai one day.

The city's inhabitants, especially foreigners who still lived there after the end of the Occupation, feared the CCP's professed distain for everything Western and everything modern. Their fear was well-founded.

The very nature of the city itself was anathema to the CCP — Shanghai was too Western to be Chinese and too Chinese to be Western. It represented a century of humiliation for China imposed by occupying foreign powers since China's defeat in the first Opium War in the 1840s.

Even the Bund, Shanghai's famous waterfront business area, with its granite-faced banks, hotels, and clubs, looked more like a postcard from Europe than it did a typical Chinese city's business area. The Bund's office buildings, Shanghai's hotels, its racecourse, and its luxury apartment buildings all screamed *modern* — a term that represented everything Mao and the CCP stood against in their peasant, countryside uprising.

Panic filled the streets of Shanghai when, on January 31, 1949, word spread that the People's Liberation Army had seized Peking and its nearby port city of Tientsin. Now, there was nothing to keep Mao and his army out of Shanghai.

On the night of May 24, the Communists shelled the city with artillery. The skies above the Bund lit up. The headline of the Shanghai edition of the *New York Times* for May 25, read, "Red Troops Enter Shanghai, Seize West, Central Areas; Nationalist Forces Flee."

The clamor for civilians to escape Shanghai became so intense that the China National Aviation Corporation suspended its flight schedules and permitted passengers to board awaiting aircraft immediately. Planes took off as soon as they were filled with fleeing Shanghailander passengers.

In late 1948, the United States lost confidence in Chiang, and began withdrawing its troops from China. It withheld materials, weapons, and financial support from the Nationalists.

Chiang was undeterred.

He believed he could defeat Mao in one decisive battle if given the opportunity. He committed his troops to that end, but he was sorely mistaken. In the autumn of 1948, the CCP defeated the Nationalists at the Battle of Liaohsi, fought in Manchuria.

In November of that same year, the CCP attacked Chiang's army who were defending China's central plain. The battle (called the Battle of Huai-hai) lasted two months, ending January 10, 1949, with the complete defeat of Chiang's army.

In the last days of the battle, Chiang ordered his air force to bomb his own troops to prevent supplies and weapons from falling into the hands of the People's Liberation Army.

The outcome of the Chinese Civil War no longer was in doubt to any objective observer. The People's Liberation Army pressed forward toward Shanghai.

On January 21, 1949, Chiang was forced to step down as president of Nationalist China. In May, the generalissimo, together with Madam Chiang, boarded a DC-3 and fled to the island of Taiwan. Approximately 600,000 members of his army had already been airlifted there. Chiang controlled twenty-six naval ships and most of his air force, now both located in Taiwan. Chiang vowed to return to the Mainland one day to destroy Mao and the People's Liberation Army.

On October 1, 1949, speaking in Peking's Tiananmen Square, Mao publicly declared victory over the Nationalists and proclaimed the formation of the People's Republic of China.

Shanghai's upper and middle class had fled Shanghai as the People's Liberation Army approached. Now, ordinary people, too, had to make a choice. Should they remain in Shanghai and live under the Communist regime or should they leave Shanghai and follow Chiang to Taiwan.

Sun-jin and Mei-hua, too, had to choose.

CHAPTER 62

Sun-jin

"**W**E MUST MAKE A DECISION" I said. "Every day we delay puts us in grave danger. The radio says the People's Liberation Army will soon be in Shanghai."

"*Ayeeyah!* I know, I know," Mai-hua said. "It's just so difficult to think about uprooting our lives and following my parents to Taiwan."

I shook my head. We'd had this discussion so many times in the past few weeks, but never with any resolution.

"It's not ideal," I said, "but staying on the Mainland is not a realistic choice. Your parents' KMT affiliation, as well as my own investigation for Chiang four years ago, eventually will come back to haunt us once the CCP has consolidated its control over Shanghai. It will only be a matter of time before we are arrested."

"But Taiwan would be no better," Mai-hua said. "Unlike our beloved Shanghai, Taiwan is a backwater, a primitive pit. We would hate it there. The Dwarf Bandits ruled the island for so many centuries that the Taiwanese do not even accept that they are Celestials. They think they are Dwarf Bandits, and act as if they are. They dress like Dwarf Bandits. They eat raw fish like Dwarf Bandits. They pray to strange gods. They even speak the language of the Dwarf Bandits, rather than speak Hu, Mandarin or Cantonese."

She shuttered at the thought of living among the Taiwanese and shook her head as if even describing the native island people was too much for her to bear.

"Besides," she said, "if we go to Taiwan, eventually my CCP activity when I was young will catch up with us. Then we will be in the same danger there from the KMT as we will be from the CCP if we remain on the Mainland. My profile in the CCP in its early days was too high for it not to follow me to Taiwan and not to come back to stalk us."

"I agree," I said. "For us, the apparent choice is not a choice at all. China under Mao, the CCP, and the People's Liberation Army or Taiwan under Chiang and the KMT? Each country now is a voracious dragon that will devour us if we don't leave.

"That's why," I said, "we must follow Eli's recent suggestion in his letter. We must leave our beloved China and emigrate to the United States as he did.

"Eli's description of his life in Washington sounds inviting. He said he knows important people in Chinatown, and that he will be glad to introduce us to them. I believe we can make a new start there, that we will be safe among Washington's Celestial community, with our personal histories left behind us in China.

"Eli is working as a PI with many Celestial clients. He said he has many contacts among Chinatown's business and triad communities, and that he will help us establish ourselves there. Perhaps he will even invite me to work with him in his PI firm," I said. "I hope so."

Mei-hua shook her head, but seemed resolute when she shrugged one shoulder.

"*Ayeeyah!* It will be so hard to leave everything we know and love," she said, "but I know you're right. We should go to America for the children's sake, if not for our own."

I took her hands in mine and pulled her close to me. I smiled and nodded. "Then it's settled. I will begin the process of obtaining our passports and other travel papers. We, the children, and Bik will go to America.

CHAPTER 63

Sun-jin

I T TOOK ME THREE WEEKS and much *squeeze* to obtain our passports, visas, and passenger-ship tickets. I arranged for us to sail aboard the American President Line's SS *General Washington*, a converted Second World War II United States troop-transport ship. At great expense and with much cajoling, I managed to rent a small stateroom for the four of us and Bik.

That was the easy part.

Based on what I had read in the newspapers and heard on the radio these past few weeks, getting to the ship from our home would be the most difficult and frightening part of this endeavor yet, especially for the children. The streets of Shanghai we would have to pass through from our home to the ship were controlled by chaos and crime, fear, and desperate people.

But first we had to prepare for that step.

We realized we could not take with us much that we held dear — our personal and family items and mementos such as scrapbooks, framed photographs, certain books, much of our clothing, Mei-hua's cheap jewelry, and other personal, physical objects. We also were limited by law how much cash or precious metals we could take out of the country. We had no gold or silver so precious metals weren't a problem for us, but we did have much depreciated yuan we'd been saving for many months.

I counted out the yuan, creating small, permissible piles of notes for each of us. When I reached the allowable limits for four people, Mei-hua took the excess and sewed it into the linings of our four suitcases to hide it from any official who might examine our luggage.

We packed one suitcase for each of us with the minimum needed to satisfy what Mei-hua and I naively believed — without any basis for such beliefs — we would need in America. The suitcases held all the clothing we could squeeze inside. I placed my unlicensed revolver and much ammunition on the floor next to my suitcase. I would use the gun to protect us, if necessary, as we navigated the streets on our way to the ship.

On the day we left for the ship, in addition to the clothing stuffed into the bulging suitcases, we each wore several pairs of underwear and several pairs of socks. I wore five shirts. The children each wore three.

We allowed Fen and Ji to pick one frivolous, small item important to them to put into their suitcases and take with them. We brought a rubber ball for Bik.

Sometime during the night before we left home, a tragedy occurred.

Mei-hua and I were awakened near sunup by the sound of Ji wailing. We ran to the children's bedroom. Ji was sitting on the floor by his bed, next to Bik, crying. Fen quietly sat on her bed, reserved for once in her life, staring at Ji and Bik.

It did not take a close-up examination by me to know that Bik had died in her sleep during the night. Her body clearly was rigid. I was sad, but not surprised. She was not a young dog. She likely had been two or three years old when we met in 1935. Now she would be fifteen or sixteen.

Mei-hua took the children to the kitchen and closed the door while I wrapped Bik's body in a blanket. I carried her to the back of our apartment building and dug a shallow grave near a plum tree. I lowered Bik and her shroud into the hole. Then I filled it in. I placed an attractive rock I found nearby on her grave.

On the morning we left, we stood briefly outside our home and all looked up at our fourth-floor apartment. One by one we said goodbye out loud to our old lives in Shanghai. The children were subdued. My voice broke as I said goodbye. Mei-hua wiped tears from her eyes.

I patted my right trouser pocket, both comforted by the presence of my revolver and disturbed that I might need to use it as we made our way to the ship.

Taxicabs had all but disappeared in Shanghai. Such little fuel as was available had become too expensive for them to acquire. Motorized taxis had been replaced by three-wheeled pedicab cycles that were propelled by strong young men.

We hailed two pedicabs — one for us and one for our luggage. We loaded our suitcases, children, and ourselves onto the vehicles, and left our home forever as the pedicab drivers, each with one pantleg rolled up above his knee, stood on the peddles, pressed down their weight, and set off for the Whangpoo Wharf where the SS *General Washington* was docked.

CHAPTER 64

Sun-jin

T HE TRIP ACROSS THE CITY to the ship was agonizingly slow and noisy. The trip frightened the children. We held them tightly, securely, against us.

Chaos ruled the streets. I sorely missed the days in the 1930s and early 1940, before the occupation by the Dwarf Bandits, when bearded Sikhs in clean white suits and bright orange turbans stood on boxes in the middle of every major intersection and directed traffic. Today, every street corner was mired in congested and often stuck pedestrian, rickshaw, and pedicab traffic, with no Sikhs to be seen.

We lost precious time at every intersection. It seemed everyone in Shanghai was in a frenzy to escape the imminent arrival of the Communists. Even though we had left home very early in the day, we worried we might not make it to the wharf in time to board the ship before it sailed.

Our young pedicab peddlers, one immediately behind the other, bulled their way through the narrow streets and intersections and through the crush of pedestrians. They shouted, cursed, and leaned on their screeching electric-battery bicycle horns as they slowly, but inexorably, moved our peddled vehicles toward the wharf. Our pedicabs bumped into rickshaws, bicycles, and pedestrians alike, often with brutal outcomes, but they did not stop.

I patted my right pocket and felt the presence of my revolver. Its presence gave me a small measure of comfort.

As we came within sight of the Astor House Hotel, we saw the ship's smokestacks. We were almost there.

Finally, we reached the wharf. I was grateful I had not needed to use my revolver.

Shipping agents, who were gathered at the foot of the ship's gangway, smoked thick cigars and shouted orders to long columns of strong men of indeterminate ages, who were stooped over by impossibly heavy loads they carried on their backs. These dock coolies — shirtless and otherwise clad only in loose, dirty rags — lugged large crates of household goods, sea trunks, and overstuffed suitcases up the ship's steep gangway.

We unloaded ourselves and our suitcases from the pedicabs and joined the long line of passengers waiting to have their papers and possessions checked by one of six immigration officers sitting behind a long, narrow table. We would be required to show our tickets, passports, and exit visas to seemingly indifferent civil servants, who would check them for legitimacy. Our suitcases might be searched for precious metals, excess yuan, and other contraband.

The *General Washington* blasted its piercing baritone horn, both startling and elating us. The children pushed themselves close into us and held on tightly.

After about twenty minutes in line, we arrived at the immigration officers' table. The officer in front of us snatched the papers from my hand, looked them over quickly, then eyeballed me, Mei-hua, the twins, and our suitcases. After a few silent, worrisome seconds, he reached for his chop, applied red ink to its end, and stamped our passports and exit visas. We had made it past the last barrier to our flight from Shanghai.

We quickly climbed the steep gangway onto the *General Washington*. Mei-hua and I carried the children's suitcases, as well as our own. The children walked behind us, both holding onto my belt as if their lives depended on it. We went directly to our cramped, small, but private stateroom, threw the four suitcases, unopened, onto the two beds, then left and made our way to the top deck and to the railing facing the Bund. We would watch our homeland slowly recede from sight as the ship pulled out into the river.

Twenty minutes passed. After three blasts of its horn, the ship slowly moved away from the wharf, churning the Whangpoo's muddy water, and headed toward the Yangtze River, then onward to the open sea.

Many passengers around us were ebullient, glad to be aboard this Round-Eyes' vessel, leaving the threat of Shanghai and the Communists behind. Others seemed depressed in their silence. Some cheered and shouted. Others were subdued. Many waved to onlookers still on the dock.

I stared across the river at the Bund, and watched as the granite facade of the Victorian-style British consulate, the neo-classical Customs House, and the clock tower atop the post office building, slipped away from view.

I was greatly relieved that Mei-hua, the twins, and I now were safe from the threat of the CCP, but I was not at all sure how I felt about what the future might hold for us in our new home.

CHAPTER 65

Sun-jin

Aboard the SS General Washington

T HE WHANGPOO WAS A DANGEROUS river to travel. We were warned by the ship's crew to remain in our cabin to avoid becoming targets for shore batteries of the People's Liberation Army, who randomly fired their weapons at passing vessels.

Years of warfare had also, in other ways, turned the Whangpoo into a harrowing passage as we headed toward the Yangtze River, itself also now a dangerous waterway. During the war against the Dwarf Bandits, the KMT had sunk surplus ships in both rivers to block the enemy's advance. When the Dwarf Bandits took over China's coast, the Dwarf Bandits mined both rivers. As the end of the Second World War approached in 1945, American air squadrons dropped hundreds of mines into both rivers to hinder the Japanese. Then, after the war, the KMT followed suit to stop Mao's army from advancing.

Shortly before we got underway, the captain announced that the People's Liberation Army had successfully fought its way to the north shore of the Yangtze River, just where we were heading on our way to the East China Sea. Once we entered the Yangtze, he said, the ship would have to run the gauntlet of live mines and shore batteries willing to fire at us. He said that our safe passage along the Whangpoo and Yangtze rivers was far from assured, but that this was not a problem for him. He said he was a very experienced seaman and would take us safely to the open sea.

I knew the captain spoke the truth about the danger to us.

Five months before we sailed, the passenger ship SS *Jiangya,* carrying three thousand passengers, most of them rich and powerful landowners and merchants, hit a mine in the Whangpoo, exploded, and sank shortly after leaving Shanghai for Taiwan. Everyone on board drowned or burned to death in the oil-soaked waters of the Whangpoo. A few weeks later, one thousand people drowned or burned to death in another maritime disaster when the SS *Taiping* hit a mine and exploded.

There was no hiding the memory of these disasters from us as we threaded our way along the two rivers. Every newspaper and newsreel in Shanghai had carried the stories, so that we passengers, on board the *General Washington,* were aware of the dangers we courted on these river journeys.

But no one on board spoke of these disasters and the possibility that we, too, might wind up at the bottom of one of the rivers, drowned or burned to death, or that we might be shot by shore batteries as we passed by. It was considered bad *joss* to mention these possibilities, but our silence did not erase them from our memories.

We were ordered to stay in our cabins and to keep away from portholes. We obeyed the orders.

When finally our ship left the Yangtze and entered the East China Sea, the captain announced that he would like everyone to meet on the top deck. He said he had an announcement to make.

We assembled at the back of the ship. The captain told us we were safe now, that we had left the dangerous rivers.

Everyone, including Ji and Fen, broke into cheers of relief. We finally were safe, and we were on our way to America.

Mei-hua, the twins, and I had ended one chapter in our lives and are about to start another. In so doing, we left behind a familiar, but hostile world. Soon, we would enter into a new world, one that will be alien to us, perhaps even hostile — a new chapter in our lives of shifting worlds that we will have to quickly learn to navigate if we are to survive and thrive.

THE END

GLOSSARY

CCP	Abbreviation for Communist Party of China
Celestial	Term used by the Chinese to laud themselves as persons who are at the center of the universe
Dwarf Bandit	Mocking phrase used by the Chinese to describe the Japanese
Green Gang	A criminal triad organization based in Shanghai, headed by Big-Eared Tu. This triad had branches around the world, including in New York City and Washington, DC
KMT	Common abbreviation to refer to the Kuomintang's army
Kuomintang	The name of the Nationalist political party headed by president Chiang Kai-shek
Kwantung	The official name of the army of Japan
Occidental	The slang name in China for a person from the West

People's Liberation Army	The name of Mao's army once he proclaimed the founding of the People's Republic of China
People's Republic of China	Name given to China when he declared victory for the CCP against the Kuomintang
Triad	A Chinese criminal and benevolent organization
Xi'an Agreement	A temporary treaty entered into between Mao Tse-tung and Chiang Kai-shek in which they agreed to stop fighting each other until, together, they had defeated the Japanese invaders

PLEASE REVIEW *FLEEING THE DRAGON* ON AMAZON

If you enjoyed **FLEEING THE DRAGON**, please post a review on Amazon at **www.Amazon.com**. Search for the book review page under my name or under the book's title, **FLEEING THE DRAGON**.

DOWNLOAD A FREE COPY OF STEVE'S FIRST MYSTERY
MANDARIN YELLOW
A Socrates Cheng mystery

Click or enter this link into your web browser:
http://www.stevenmroth.com/FreeBook.aspx

Visit me at www.StevenMRoth.com to see all of my published books and receive information about my upcoming books

ACKNOWLEDGEMENTS

First, of course, my thanks to Dominica who, as always, both encouraged me to write and then supported my efforts in many, many ways.

I am fortunate to have had several people who acted as my early reading team — reading the manuscript before it was finalized and tearing into several parts of it, forcing me to re-think several scenes and chapters, and, of course, correcting my mistakes. For their great help, I thank: Penny Campbell-Myhill, Peter J. Harding, Patricia A. Kaufmann, Thomas M. Lera, Linda Nejame, and Charla Niche.

I also thank Dr. Wayne Weiner, a terrific author (who writes in his Masada 2 thriller series under the nom de plume, Dr. Zev Goldman Weiner) for his assistance with Chapter 40.

BIOGRAPHY

Steven M. Roth has written (i) a three-book contemporary mystery series featuring his Washington, DC, half-Chinese, half-Greek American private eye — Socrates Cheng; (ii) a two-book suspense series featuring ex-Navy SEAL, Trace Austin; and, (iii) a four-book historical mystery set in 1930s – 1940s Shanghai. He currently is working on the fifth book in his Shanghai series.

The first book in Steve's Socrates Cheng mystery series — MANDARIN YELLOW — is available free to download at http://www.stevenmroth.com/FreeBook.htm

Visit Steve's web site (www.stevenmroth.com) for more information about his existing books and to sign-up for his occasional newsletters giving information about his upcoming books.

Made in the USA
Middletown, DE
26 April 2022

64669004R00158